A BULLIED REUNION

Chris Ponici

A Bullied Reunion
Copyright © 2018 by Chris Ponici

All rights reserved. No part of this publication may be reproduced, distributed, or transmitted in any form or by any means, including photocopying, recording, or other electronic or mechanical methods, without the prior written permission of the author, except in the case of brief quotations embodied in critical reviews and certain other non-commercial uses permitted by copyright law.

Tellwell Talent
www.tellwell.ca

ISBN
978-1-77370-828-7 (Hardcover)
978-1-77370-827-0 (Paperback)
978-1-77370-829-4 (eBook)

A BULLIED REUNION

To Sue,
my first and only love.

To Dobre Leuca,
my eternal force.

"First learn to become invincible, then wait for your enemy's moment of vulnerability."
Sun Tzu

Prelude

There is no greater high than the moment just before you kill a human being.

When you are in complete control of another man's destiny.

No drug. No sexual exploit. No thrill or sport or event can prepare you for the surge of adrenaline that courses through your being as you point a 9mm, nickel-plated Beretta at the head of your childhood bully and he looks at you with eyes of despair and loss. Defeat exits his retinal cave as he shakes and soils himself. He begs for his life with every cell in his destroyed body; he asks for forgiveness, but none will come.

Your finger hovers over the trigger.

The chasm between this world and the next is separated only by one small, four-pound pull that will end one life and forever change another. Because once you have stepped into the world of murder, you never come back the same, if at all. You have *taken* a life.

The desperation in the eyes of my victim mirror my own. The panic and dread and mortification that consume him have walked the halls of my heart and slept in my soul.

And then the release…. The flash and click of gunpowder explodes in a chamber of guided murder, the bullet spiraling toward the target. Finding its fleshy home of muscle and membrane. Giving of itself as it takes from another.

CHAPTER 1:

Grade 8
(1992-1993)

"Have a good day, sweetie," my mom said as she parked the car. She leaned over and tried to kiss me on the cheek; an eastern European habit, I guess.

"Mom, come on, please," I objected.

Saddened, she continued, "Be your best today, ok?" Her accent was almost gone. Night school and Saturday classes erased a history and heritage once revealed in her voice.

"I will." I reached around to the back seat and grabbed my pack. "I'll take the bus home after school, so you don't have to pick me up. I'm gonna hang out with Alex."

The bell screamed at us to get our asses to class.

"Cristiano Leuca," Mrs. Zimmer called out.

I raised a reluctant hand. "Here."

"Dipesh Ranjit," she said, going down her list; roll call.

"Here."

It was our high school orientation and the gymnasium was filled with eager and afraid teens who sat cross-legged on the floor. Murmurs and nervous giggles bounced off backboards. Girls talked about their summer crushes; boys of squished bugs and captured snakes.

But Alex and I sat silently, no words. Until, that is, the boy behind her pulled on her bra strap through her shirt and snapped it back.

"Hey, fuck off!" she said, turning around to slap the young offender. Her shout interrupted Mrs. Zimmer, and every single student now looked Alex's way.

"Is there a problem?" Mrs. Zimmer asked.

"No, sorry," replied Alex, the ever-faithful one who wouldn't even rat out an enemy.

Mrs. Zimmer—who looked older than Moses and probably lived through the Great Depression, two world wars, and numerous horrible sexual experiences—said, "I don't condone swearing, missy. Now off you go, down to the Principal's office." She fluttered her hand toward the side door of the gym.

"I said I'm sorry—" Alex started, but it was of no use.

"Tell it to Mr. Price." Mrs. Zimmer looked back at her list. "Steve Williamson…"

Alex walked toward the exit.

I love Alex—as a friend, of course. Nothing at all sexual about our relationship. And not because I was too young to really care about sex; no, not at all. I mean, I masturbated every morning and after school, and usually three solid times on Saturday. It was like taking a piss; it was something my body needed to do. I hadn't kissed a girl yet and, at thirteen, I didn't want to, either. Comic books and candy stores were my first love.

Alex turned around just before she reached the door and gave me a quick wink. I could see why all my friends thought she was hot: she had the body and brains of a seventeen-year-old. Her dark red hair looked like it was bathed in the morning dew. She wore a jean skirt without any leggings that flaunted the whitest skin you ever laid eyes on. And her black, short-sleeve top did nothing to hide her budding, perky little breasts. Alex was a year older than most of us: she moved here from Hungary four years ago, and started school later than the rest of society usually does. She grew up on a farm, and when she turned six her mother got terribly sick, so her father ended up doing pretty much everything that needed to be done (whatever farm people do). And so she never went to school that year; she stayed around the house and kept her mom company, I guess. She never really talks about—

"Hey, lover boy," a voice behind me called. "Guess your little bitch got in trouble."

Before I had a chance to turn around, I heard a *pffft* and felt a cold, chunky glob of spit hit my neck. Laughter ensued behind me.

"Settle down over there!" Mrs. Zimmer yelled.

I froze. I couldn't move. Stunned. Shocked. Unable to formulate my next thought.

What the fuck was I supposed to do? Wipe the back of my neck? With what? All I had was a T-shirt and jeans. Nothing in my pocket and nothing—

"Mrs. Zimmer?" I raised my hand. "I need to go to the bathroom."

She was done calling out names on her list. "You just got here," she replied. "Can it wait?"

I reluctantly nodded and plotted my next move.

Kids behind me snickered. Whispers of "Ugh, gross" and "Oh, my, god, look at that." The globular muck of snot and phlegm made its way from the back of my neck to under my shirt. It was enough of a gagging sight that those around felt it necessary to continue observing.

Nevertheless, I was not going to show my displeasure to anyone. I would deal with this in my own way, like I usually do: by backing down and scurrying away physically and mentally.

I wasn't much of a fighter, you see. I've only really been in two good scraps, and they ended with me beaten and bruised. Both times someone took something that was mine and it set me off. But I've learned my lesson: my body was not designed for combat; it was made for more intellectual pursuits.

The slippery, snotty slime was now at the centre of my back. All I could think of was to press on it with my shirt and make a circular motion with my hand (I know, I know, not the best idea, but you make do with what you got). I wiped it around until I could feel that most of it was absorbed into my shirt and then left it alone. "That. Is. So. Fucking. Nasty," a girl behind me said. I could have crawled into the gym floor and buried myself.

Mrs. Zimmer asked everyone to go to the tables on the far side of the gym where we'd receive our locker assignments and class schedules. As I began to stand, somebody pushed me while I was barely half-way up, so I ended up on my ass.

It was going to be a *long* morning…

"Hey," I said, "how'd the office visit go?"

"Never went," Alex replied.

We stood next to my locker on the first floor in what seemed like one of those massive hallways in space stations you see in sci-fi films.

"What? Are you serious?" I couldn't believe the guts on this girl.

"She won't remember shit. She's as old as the fucking Bible."

"So…who's your locker partner? I still haven't seen mine," I said.

"You're lookin' at her," she said while doing a little mock curtsy.

"For real? What are the chances of that?"

She leaned in close: "See that homeboy standing over there?" A lean black kid to my right was messing around with the combo on his locker. "I said I'd give him a hand-job after school if he switched with me."

"You're really fucked up, ya know?" I smiled. I was happy I'd at least be spending the first year of high school with her close by. Then, confused, I said, "How'd you know *he* was gonna be *my* locker partner?"

"I'm not just a pretty face, *ya know?*"

Another bell rang, and a voice came over the speaker system that instructed all Grade 8 students to make their way to their block "A" classes.

I was glad this was only a half day. Find our classrooms, grab a seat (and it better be a good one, 'cause your stuck with it for the whole semester), meet new teachers, get textbooks, and head home at noon.

"Come on," Alex said, "you don't wanna be late."

Mr. Beasley was his name and Science 8 was his game. Or so he rapped to us as we all sat down at our desks. He had the curliest hair I ever saw on a man—short and bouncy and would make the great Shirley Temple envious.

He walked around the class handing out our textbooks for the year while discussing how much fun we were going to have exploring the "wondrous world of science!" He explained the various topics and chapters we were going to cover; how we were the first class in the twenty-five-year history of BCSS to finally get approval from the school board to dissect a sheep's heart, and how "happy and delighted" he was to have this inaugural opportunity.

What happened next marked me for the rest of my life…

I was seated in the third row. My Chicago Bulls binder teetered near the edge of the desk and when Mr. Beasley walked by and slammed the textbook down on top of my binder, both tumbled to the floor. My binder spilled open and exposed a Platinum Edition Spider-Man comic book, a few Upper Deck basketball cards, and—to the horror of everyone, including yours truly—a picture of Mayim Bialik from TV's *Blossom*, completely naked, stroking her clitoris with legs spread wide! Some fucking idiot had pasted a picture of her head from a teen magazine and glued it to this pornographic image of a woman vigorously pleasing herself. (It must have been left in the textbook on purpose, for such a time as this…)

"Well…it looks like we have a *Blossom* fan on our hands," Mr. Beasley said as he picked up the offending photo. He was kind enough to leave the textbook and my binder on the floor while he inspected the evidence.

"It's not mine," I said.

"Really? That's too bad; it's quite inventive." He would not look away from the picture. He just stared and devoured it. His moustache and glasses quivered. Fucking guy probably hasn't seen snatch like that since he was—

"Hey, Blossom," someone called out near the back. "Can you make me one of those?" The class erupted in nervous laughter. "Maybe one with your mom!" Another small roar.

"All right—shut it off. Enough," Mr. Beasley interjected, making a cutting motion with his hand. He slipped the picture ever so discreetly into his shirt pocket while he walked back to his desk to retrieve the last few textbooks. (Most teachers asked a couple of students to do this monotonous task, but he took just a second longer every few desks to ogle a pretty girl and flash a creepy smile.) "You'll see a sign-out card pasted on the inside front cover. I need you to print your first and last name and date it."

"B-L-O-S-S-O-M," a student behind me said as he jabbed me in the back with a pencil.

"F-A-G-G-O-T," an asshole to the right said. Then: "H-O-M-O," from my left.

∗   ∗   ∗

"Are you serious?" Alex said when I told her of my science situation. "That really happened?"

"I swear," I said. "Fuckin' picture fell right outta the damn textbook; everyone thought it was mine."

"Hey, at least you have taste. That Blossom chick's pretty cute."

Alex always found the silver lining. We headed to our next class. I said, "I just hope—"

"Hey, Blossom, got any more pictures of your girlfriend?" I heard someone say as they passed… And this is where it stuck. This is where I realized that for the next five or so years "Blossom" would be my nickname.

"Hey—I was talkin' to you—" the same prick said.

"Go fuck your fat mom," Alex said.

We kept walking.

"Fuck you, cunt!" This guy would not let up.

We stopped walking. I knew what was coming next, so I said, "Listen, bro, it's all good…"

"The fuck it is," he said. "You and your bitch better learn some fuckin' manners."

A bunch of students stopped what they were doing and gathered around us. The florescent lights buzzed overhead, and the clock ticked in one of the alcoves.

"And I ain't your 'bro,' loser." I had no idea what grade the piece of shit was in. But as he approached me he seemed to get bigger with every step. I mean, I probably only weighed about a hundred pounds (fully clothed), but this beast was easily one-fifty. And not fat, either. He towered over us like a bridge troll.

Ah, my dear Alex; my saviour, my everything. The one I can count on when all is going oh so wrong. She always seemed to have the words, the wisdom, the vile vocabulary to put everyone in their place. But this time, I wish that my dearest, bestest, awesomest friend would have just let it go. We must choose our battles. And we just chose the wrong one.

"What? You not man enough? You need your bitch over there to fight your battles?" He was right in my face. Stinky breath and all.

Then it happened: Alex came between us, ever so calmly, grabbed him by the shoulders—they were almost the same height, give or take a quarter inch—stared deeply into his eyes and smiled. I knew what was coming, but all big boy could say was, "You gonna kiss me now?" And then, in the swiftest of motions, she yanked down on his shoulders while kneeing him in the balls with all the force she could muster.

"Ahhh, ohhhhh, ohhhhh…" he moaned as he dropped to the ground, clutching his testicles. He coughed a couple of times and his face turned bright red. He whimpered and rocked from side to side and then slowly he tucked himself into the fetal position.

"Oh, look at the poor baby," Alex mocked, standing over him. "He's all hurt. Are you okay, little baby?" She stood over him for a moment before she crouched down and tilted her head to the right, so she could be face to face. She tapped his forehead with her finger. "Don't ever talk to us again, got it?"

The second bell rang. We were all supposed to be in our last class of the day. But nobody moved. We all stood still, portrait-like, and watched this young girl rise, confidence spilling out of every pore. Unafraid; completely in control.

She grabbed my elbow—like a family member would do to a child—and said: "Don't come back to your locker. Just finish the day and we'll meet at the bus stop."

(I knew that Alex wanted to be a cop, just like her uncle and grandfather were back in Hungary. She did junior policing camp this past summer with the Vancouver Police Department and vowed that she would head straight to the recruiting office after graduating. What just happened solidified that fucking with her was trouble. She was known as the "Hungarian from Hell" from then on.)

"…Mr. Leuca? You there? Hello?"

I snapped awake from my thoughts; daydreaming. Mr. Lewiston was about five feet from my desk. He had asked me a direct question that I did not hear and probably did not know the answer to.

"Sorry," I said, "I wasn't listening."

"What book did you enjoy you reading this summer?" he asked. His arms were crossed, and his right eyebrow was raised. He disliked me already.

"Well…" I took a big pause, unsure of myself. "I just finished reading *American Psycho*." It sounded like more of a question than an answer.

"Never heard of it." He turned around and walked to the front of the class. "What was it about?"

I scanned the room. They looked at me as though I had a third eye. "Uh, well, it's about this guy who's a banker during the day and kills people at night." I swallowed hard.

"Sounds intriguing," Mr. Lewiston said.

"Yeah, it's weird, and tough to digest, but overall, really good."

"And how many books would you say you read this summer? You sound like quite the critic."

What the hell was going on? Fuck! Why did I have to doze off...now I'm fodder for this fucker. "I read a few. I like to read on the beach."

"So does my mom," Jeremy Freemont said. And the whole class laughed.

I started to see a pattern here: I speak, people mock. Real nice...

Mr. Lewiston asked again: "How many *exactly* did you read this summer?"

I thought he would let it go and move on, but I struck some sort of nerve with this guy. I guess he doesn't appreciate kids zoning out in class.

"I dunno"—I didn't want to sound like a geek, but I also wanted to impress, to show him that my blankness earlier was a misstep that wouldn't happen again—"I usually read, like, two books a week or so."

"So that's, *like*—" he enunciated mockingly, "sixteen books in one summer. Pretty impressive." He took a step back and sat on the edge of his big wooden desk. He was bald on top with gray hair on the sides connected to a full salt-and-pepper beard. His belly folded over his belted corduroys. "Do you write at all?"

I squirmed in my seat, completely uncomfortable with this line of questioning from an English 8 teacher. His tone was snobbish and condescending, like he had some point to prove.

All I could say was, "I like to journal every night." (Big mistake.)

"You and my mom could be best friends!" Jeremy Freemont said.

Eruption of laughter. Teacher doing fuck all, a diabolical look on his face.

"How do you know we're not?" I said, cleverly trying to disarm the laughter.

"Oooohhhhhh..." said the class in one accord.

"Yeah, we'll see, Blossom Boy,"

Wow. Again with the *Blossom*. At this point, it was probably broadcast all the way to the Yukon.

"Actually, it's just 'Blossom,' you don't need the boy part..." I shook my head in disgust. "...idiot." I knew that my rebuttal didn't do anything to strengthen my case, but it was the only thing that came out. You would think, though, with all the words and characters I had devoured over the years that I would have something snappier to say; a comeback with a little more *umph*. But, to be honest, I wasn't in the mood. I'd been in high school for less than three hours and it was already turning into a mess. I had no guy friends to speak of; I was pretty much the smallest, skinniest kid in the entire school—which is horrible, seeing as there were around twelve hundred students. And now my nickname was based on a TV show featuring the girliest of girly-girls who was named after a cluster of flowers.

The teacher yapped away about the books we were going to read, the writing assignments, and the tests and essays we would write. He left me alone and did not look my way once the entire time. Jeremy Freemont, though, eye-fucked me for the rest of the class. But I'm not sure why. In my best estimation, he won that round. I mean, I basically emasculated myself in front of everyone when I corrected him. I probably even did it on purpose. I wanted him to see that my self-sabotage was a way of apologizing for the mom comment. Fuck, I should've been listening to Mr. Lewiston talking right now, but my heart was pounding, and I felt scared. What would happen when the bell rang and I was forced to face two giants?

It made me wonder if my mother fed me enough. I was pretty even with most kids my age in grades 6 and 7, but it seemed as though everyone else hit a growth spurt over the summer. [My dad would later say that "they put hormones and steroids in fast food"; that kids drink too much milk which is filled with sugar and additives—and would go into a massive dialogue about the dangers of pasteurization {he held a degree in both chemistry and biology and, to be fair, was way ahead of his time when it came to healthcare}; and how nothing was really farm fresh anymore].)

"You really don't like to be present in the *here* and *now*, do you?"

Shit. Mr. Lewiston hovered over my right shoulder. The class had pretty much emptied. The bell must have rung a while ago. "I'm really sorry. I *was* listening—I heard everything, I swear."

"Good. Good for you." He turned around and grabbed his briefcase, looked back toward me, shook his head, and left the classroom.

*　*　*

After school, there was a pack of about sixty kids waiting for the bus at the stop across the street. I approached slowly and cautiously and looked to see if I recognized anyone. I didn't spot Alex and hated that I had no one to stand with. More students approached from behind, filling in around me. *Maybe my mom should have picked me up*, I thought. Even though I knew I had to get used to taking public transit every day from now on, it still would have been nice to get out as soon as possible.

"Hey," Alex said as she approached. "It's pretty packed, huh?"

"Yeah...Where you been?" I asked.

"Mrs. Zimmer caught me in the hallway. She gave me a big lecture about swearing. She actually thinks I went and saw the principal."

Students filled in tight around us. There were probably a good hundred that waited. Out of the corner of my eye I finally spotted the *120 Vancouver* that would take us down Canada Way through the suburbs of Burnaby and on to New Westminster. A twenty-minute trip, depending on traffic. As the bus pulled up, there were already quite a few passengers on board, so I knew we would have to wait for the next one.

"Shit," Alex said. "Come on, try to squeeze in."

There was standing room only and I could see the line almost to the front. "We won't make this one," I said. "There's, like, ten people ahead of us." Alex pushed me a little from behind. "Hey!"

"Just squish in," she whispered. "We'll make it."

Alex's determination worked. We got on. Even though I stood just above the stairwell, the driver was none too happy about us being in "front of the red line"—the one BC Transit deemed to be some sort of safety boundary—but he let it go. (You see, as much as we wanted to take the big yellow school bus, it did not, unfortunately, travel south of the school. It only serviced the northern suburbs of Burnaby; so, the rest of us who lived below Canada Way and Deer Lake Parkway [the school's intersection] had to contend with public transportation to get to and from school.)

As we pulled away I watched the massive structure that was to be my prison for the next five years fade away into the distance. Ironically, I found out later that it actually *was* a prison constructed to house the criminally insane back in the early '40s. It was remodeled in 1975 and turned into a high school. The inside was completely renovated. The concrete structure was three floors high and about one and a half football fields long, with two gymnasiums, countless classrooms, a massive playing field. There was also a tower on the far north corner that was used as a lookout for potential escapees back in the day but now sheltered the school bell.

I steadied myself as the bus picked up speed. I took in a deep breath. If this was just Day One, what the hell would the rest of the year bring?

Alex bumped me with her backpack. "See, I told you we'd make it."

* * *

Unless you really cared or looked for it, you would probably miss our little grey house on the corner of Canada Way and Tenth Avenue. It was over fifty years old and smelled like a hundred. It was built on the Burnaby side of the New West/Burnaby border directly across the street from another hell-hole called New Westminster Secondary School (NWSS). An East Indian couple with two elementary school children bought the property on our right, tore down the house, and erected their own mini-Taj. (This was typical of our neighborhood: crack houses next to newly-built, single family homes.) A wild bunch of bikers who consumed booze and broads every Friday and Saturday night until the wee hours of the morning lived on our left. A colourful assortment of tattooed thugs, paraded in and out laughing and jostling one another. They revved their Harleys and sped away at all hours of the night on beer runs with their "old ladies' " boobies squishing up against them from behind. But all things considered, they were good to have next door: nobody with criminal intentions *ever* came around our street. We never had a break-in, a stolen vehicle, vandalism, or other petty crimes that plagued the rest of the street. During the winter on those rare occasions when it snowed, they would pay me $20 to shovel their driveway and front walk. My father, the ever-present fear factory, did not like my interaction with said individuals and would always admonish me to stay away.

I always came and went through the rear of the house. I took the alley that snaked around to Canada Way. Tenth Avenue was a constant hustle of traffic that started early and ended late (nobody needed an alarm clock in my house—the horns blared and honked at 6:00 a.m. and wouldn't let up till 6:00 p.m.; twelve hours of non-stop vehicular pandemonium). After a car jumped the curb and killed a kid while he was riding his bike a few years back, I never set foot anywhere near the main road.

My tiny bedroom was in the basement—well, it was sort of a basement; I was half in/half out: the window in my room was level with the ground, so I could see what the ants and worms saw, but the rest was subterranean. I spent most of my time there playing Nintendo, PC video games on my Intel Pentium 486, reading sci-fi/fantasy novels, and watching *Star Trek: The Next Generation* (and *Blossom*, occasionally, too…). But right now, I wasn't doing any of those things. Right now, I was hungry. Famished. I had only eaten Lucky Charms with extra marshmallows and a banana around 7:30 a.m., and a strawberry Fruit Roll-Up around 10:00 a.m. So, I sauntered up the rickety, decrepit wooden stairs to the kitchen where I could satiate myself to my heart's content.

My mom was asleep on the couch with the television on disturbingly loud. A bottle of vodka (a third of it empty), and an orange juice-stained glass rested comfortably close on the coffee table. She was still in her pink cotton bathrobe—the same one she drove me to school in this morning—and her short black hair looked depressingly greasy, like she hadn't washed it in over a week. It didn't look like anything was cooked or baked in the kitchen since this morning, so it was another screwball breakfast with *Regis and Kathie Lee*; another morning where my three-year-old sister, Lucia, who was nowhere to be seen, would have to fend for herself.

I walked over to the TV, turned it down, switched it to a cartoon network, and set out to find my little sis. It shouldn't be too hard because our kitchen and living room were essentially the same, and all that was left was a modest bathroom in between two bedrooms. It took about thirty seconds to scan the whole house and conclude that my sister was not in it. (My grandparents lived a few blocks south in New West; they probably took her to the park, knowing my mother's daily routine of drink and depression.)

So…with my dad at work, my mom drunk on the couch, and my sister with the grandfolks, I was pretty much alone. Nobody to ask me how my first half day at school went; nobody to care about the abuse and intimidation I received today…NOBODY. If my mom was sober, though, I knew she'd want to hear all about it and try to do or say something to make me feel better. She liked to talk and talk and talk. Very little action. My dad, on the other hand, was the complete opposite: all action, no talk. But his actions always seemed to be wrong and directed toward me with a slap, a fist, or a belt for the smallest childhood infractions. And if I tried to tell him about what happened, he'd ask me what I did to either provoke or stop the harassment. That would be his philosophy: I must have done *something* to instigate the bullying; if not, then I must do *something* to end it. Because, you see, he wanted me to be this proverbial tough guy, like he thought he was when he was younger, but I didn't have the physical constitution for what he wanted his son to look and act like. And I think that made him angry. To the point of resentment. Plus, as a Romanian refugee who escaped during Ceausescu's reign of terror, sympathy for petty things—such as bullying—was not one of his stronger attributes.

Well…since no one was around, I decided to make a bowl of macaroni and cheese and go hang out in my room. There were a few more Spider-Man comic books that I wanted to crack open for the first time and a bunch more levels I needed to pass on *Super Mario Bros.* Just as I switched the burner on the stove to high and accidently banged a pot, my mom yawned and sat up on the couch. Her hair was staticky on one side; it made her look windswept.

"Heeeyyy…hello, my son," she said. She pushed herself up off the couch and wobbled toward me. "Give me a hug. How was your first day?" She squeezed me tight.

"It was OK," I said. I turned back to the sink and continued filling the pot with water.

"Good…do you have nice teachers?"

"Yeah, I guess." The pot was on the stove now, covered and ready to boil.

"I can do that." She grabbed the Kraft macaroni box from the upper cupboard and tore it open. "Go sit down," she added.

I grabbed a Pepsi from the fridge and took a seat at our tiny kitchen table. The cold can cracked and popped and fizzed as I opened it. (The first few sips are delicious.)

"How did Alex like it?" she asked.

"She was fine. Everybody seems to like her right away."

"Do you have any classes together?"

"No; but I think we might next semester."

"Any cute girls?"

"Mom—come on…"

"Hey, you're a big boy now"—she hugged my head from the side, pressed her bosom against my cheek; I could smell vodka and Vinete (a Romanian eggplant salad) on her breath—"you can have a girlfriend. I don't mind..."

I changed the subject. "Where's Lucia?"

"Luci? I think your grandpa took her." She called my sister "Luci" (Loo-Chee) for short.

She poured the noodles into the boiling water, turned the heat down to medium and sat down next to me with her own Pepsi. "I got another rejection letter in the mail," she said.

"That sucks," I replied.

My mother wrote poetry ever since she could remember. She was first published in her hometown of Bucharest when she was only in grade school, and then subsequently in high school, and in her university monthly newspaper. Her poems focused mainly on the beauty of the land, the freedom of the forest, and nature's power to transform and heal our souls. (I'd read some of her work...pretty good stuff.) Unfortunately, it did not translate well into English, so she suffered through rejection after rejection from all the major (and minor) literary magazines and publications in Canada.

"I don't really care anymore," she said. She looked out the window, jaw clenched.

I knew she was lying. All she ever talked about was writing and the books she read or wanted to read. My father couldn't stand it. The only things he ever read were technical manuals for the latest gizmos, computer magazines, and science textbooks or compendiums for work. No two people more different have ever gotten together in the history of mankind: my mom, an artsy-fartsy poet who writes every moment she's awake; and then my father, a technical engineer/chemist/bio-dude who talks about UFOs and how man never really landed on the moon; a man with whom I've never held a lengthy conversation with about anything remotely interesting to me or to my needs as a kid.

"Don't give up yet. It'll happen," I said.

"I have to find a job," she said, getting up to charge to the bathroom.

I could hear her vomit into the toilet. That's when I saw the open envelope on the kitchen counter with the letter from a poetry magazine in Montreal.

Some water boiled over onto the stovetop, so I stirred and then tasted a couple of noodles. They were done.

"Are you OK?" I asked once she emerged.

"Just a little under the weather," she replied. Her favourite line when she was inebriated.

"Do you want some macaroni?"

She was back at the table, staring blankly out the window. A fresh tear formed in her right eye. It slid down her cheek and a quiver appeared on her lower lip. Shy and a little embarrassed for her—(I don't see my mom cry very often but when I do, for some reason, I get all uncomfortable)—I quickly drained the water, emptied the cheese pack on top of the noodles, and stirred. I didn't bother adding any milk or butter, like I usually do. I just wanted to finish up and go to my room.

With my back turned, I mixed the powdered cheese into the macaroni. Mom hugged me from behind and kissed the top of my head.

"I'm going for a walk, but I'll be back soon," she said.

When my dad came home around four o'clock, he didn't even ask how my first day of school went. He just wanted to know where my mother was and what time we would be eating. He was famished, starved, and rambling in Romanian about how Mom is "never home" and "always doing something stupid."

"I can cook some European wieners, if you want?" I asked. I was on the couch watching highlights on MuchMusic of the Guns N' Roses: Use Your Illusion Tour. Axl was bouncing around onstage, shrieking like a hellish banshee.

"Turn it off!" my father barked. He swore in Romanian and told me to make something, quickly. God forbid he cooks for himself…

He yanked the remote out of my hand and flipped the channel to a program about the conflict in the Middle East.

"Did she tell you where she was going?" he asked.

I knew he was frustrated because he spoke in Romanian. Because he had been using English all day, it spilled over to our household. When he was pissed off or cranky, then, suddenly he became this Romanic rooster who'd peck everything in sight until everyone around him was just as irritated and grouchy as he was.

"No. She went for a walk a few hours ago. That's all—"

The phone rang. My dad yanked it out of the cradle. It was my mom. I could tell she was asking him to come get her because he moaned about how hungry he was and that he was busy making food (yeah, right…Mom new better…). I guess she told him to pick her up after he was done.

"In an hour," he said. "But come down—I don't want to go up." (My grandparents lived in an old apartment where the elevator probably only worked once a month. He hung up, cracked open the ice-cold Michelob teardrop bottle he held in his left hand and guzzled down a quarter of it. "Hurry up."

My dad continually acted like a blue-collar bastard rather than a white lab-coat chemist. I turned the stove on and waited for the water to boil.

* * *

There were only two small clouds in the sky. Both white and fluffy, like the inside of one of my pillows, I imagined. The sun was awake with welcome intensity. I felt her heat on the back of my neck even at this early hour as I walked up the hill to the bus stop. Lower Mainland had almost non-existent winters (barely ever below zero) and mild summers (a day above thirty degrees was rare). With soccer try outs after school, the day looked like a perfect mix of sun and breeze. It was an ideal combo to showcase my brilliant footwork: not too hot where you get tired and dehydrated, and not too cold that you clam up and your leg muscles tighten like ropes being pulled around your calves and thighs.

The bus stop was packed with students. I expected maybe three or four others—mainly because that's how many students got off on yesterday's bus—but I counted at least ten. Most of them were either Asian or Spanish. There were a couple of white kids and one black guy—THE GUY! Shit. It was him! From yesterday in the gym! He's the one who snapped Alex's bra and then spat on me. Fucking hell. I quickly looked down and hoped he hadn't noticed me yet. I stood next to a couple of Filipino girls who were talking loud and fast and giggled with way too much energy for eight o'clock in the morning.

I kept my back turned and barely moved. So far so good. No contact made. But then, because Curious Cristiano just couldn't leave well enough alone, I had to turn my head to the right to check on him. And, of fucking course, we made eye contact.

He grinned. Nodded his head. Knew exactly who I was.

I turned swiftly. Bad move. I showed more weakness than an African gazelle.

He wore a black bandanna, grey baggy jeans, a white T-shirt, and a silver peace sign hanging off his neck from a leather strap. He walked—well, it looked more like a limp: that cool, bob-to-the-side-dip-my-head-down-low stride—slowly toward me.

"My nigga…look who it is," he said. He was crazy tall for an eighter. I swear this thug wannabe was left back two, maybe even three, years.

"Hey, whatsup?" was all I could muster.

"Where's your pretty little redhead?"

"She's one stop up—"

"Man, shut the fuck up! Did I tell ya to speak?"

"You asked—"

"I what!?" He was right in my face. He looked down at me; our foreheads touched. He pushed my head back with his. "Say sumthin' again. Come on, say sumthin'…"

The brakes on the *120 Vancouver* squealed and gave him pause. I could see the wheels turning in that faded afro head of his. "You take the earlier one, or you take the later. But that bus there"—he pointed with his thumb—"that's mine."

"Are you seri—"

He slapped my mouth. "Don't ever open your fucking mouth." He turned and made his way to the front of the line.

Nobody said a word. Nobody came to my rescue. I thought maybe someone would tell the bus driver as they got on, but no. Nothing for a nobody like me…

The next bus wouldn't come for fifteen minutes—at 8:32. With school starting at 8:50, I would be late. On my second day. Great.

Everybody trotted onto the bus and the driver didn't notice me. He just wanted to get the noisy bunch to school. With a puff of charcoal-coloured diesel smoke the bus took off. My new-found enemy smiled through the rear window; evil and intense.

"Glad to see you could make it," Ms. Lang said as I entered her French 8 class, late. "I hope we weren't keeping you from anything?"

"Sorry, I missed the bus," I said. I was only a few minutes late, no big deal; she just started the attendance and began to discuss her three-week trip to Montreal this past summer.

I found a seat near the far end of the class, next to a window that overlooked the courtyard. And who should I see to my right but—

"Robert Gregory Cook," Ms. Lang called out.

"It's just Rob," he answered.

"Very well, Just Rob," Ms. Lang replied. The class chuckled.

—*him*. The large-type asshole who Alex kneed in the balls yesterday! The zit-faced prick sat in the seat right beside me. He caught my stare. His buzz-cut head whipped over and said: "Whatcha lookin' at, faggot?"

Ms. Lang continued down through her class list. I didn't hear any of the names except for the boy in front of Rob—Jeremy Freemont—and the boy behind—Michael Underwood.

So, there you have it: The Terrific Trio. One whose nuts were probably still sore, one who pretty much labeled me for the entirety of my high school tenure as "Blossom," and one who figures he owns and directs my bus schedule.

Ms. Lang rapped on about her trip to Quebec. Nobody paid attention to the places she described and food she ate. All I could think of was switching classes.

Michael leaned forward, his ironic peace sign dangled and hit his desktop loudly. "You gonna wish you was dead, boy," he said.

Jeremy leaned back. His dirty blond hair was cut almost exactly as mine, in that Leonardo DiCaprio *Growing Pains* phase. "Gonna fuck you up, Blossom," he said.

"Is there something you would like to share with the rest of the class, Jeremy?" Ms. Lang's voice was witchy. She wore a pink, knee-high skirt with white leggings and a matching jacket over a white dress shirt. Her hair was midnight black and knife-cut straight across her forehead, like that gal who hosted *Fashion Television* (my mom watched it religiously every Sunday, that's how I know, OK?)

"I was just askin' about somethin'," Jeremy answered. "Sorry."

A BULLIED REUNION

"Close mouth, open mind," Ms. Lang said in a Zen-ish way. She approached the chalkboard and started the lesson on grammatical gender. We opened our binders and took notes. I, though, probably stared at the clock more than the board. I was impatient and still edgy from this morning's humiliating bus fiasco.

First two periods: over. French was easy enough (except for the Three Amigos who would be joining me for the rest of the semester) and Social Studies looked about as challenging as a Sunday picnic. And with Drama and P.E. after lunch, I could basically coast through the rest of the day without really having to think much.

"Where're you hangin' for lunch?" Alex asked, standing right behind me.

I tried to jam my textbook in between two binders in my locker. I wanted everything in a specific order, so I could just grab and go. "Cafeteria?" I said.

Alex nodded. "Let's go have a smoke first."

"I don't think grade eights are allowed in the smoke pit. And don't people usually smoke *after* they eat?"

"I can smoke whenever I want." She turned on her heel and I faithfully followed...

...to the Cancer Pit. The Lung Locker. The Nicotine Nebula.

The filthy fumes hung above us as we stood in a semi-alcove on the eastern part of the building, right near the back. There were two white spray lines that indicated where students—Grade 10 and up, **ONLY!**—could stand and smoke. If we were any closer to the dumpsters, we'd be inside of them. The crowd was a punk/goth mix with a few token hip-hopians and Def Leppard dudes. Nobody talked. Nobody looked at each other. Alex puffed away in silence while I stood next to her with one hand in my pocket and the other one holding my brown lunch bag filled with a peanut butter and jelly sandwich, an apple, and a berry yogurt drink. No teachers had walked by yet. I was hungry and bored. Alex didn't talk when she smoked. She just sucked in and blew out. She would squint with each drag and cock her head back as she exhaled the poison.

"All right," I said, "I'm gonna go eat."

"Eat here," she said. "Fuck going inside."

I leaned my back against the green dumpster and slid down in a sort of crouching/sitting position and unfurled my bag. "If you really want to be a cop, smoking isn't the best habit."

"It's good for undercover work." She nodded her head back and forth and contemplated her next response. "Bad guys'll think I'm like them."

"Just 'cause you smoke?" My mouth was full.

This kid wearing a long, Nazi-esque trench coat with Gestapo boots looked our way and said, "You wanna be a fucking NARC?"

"Yeah, I do…" she replied, "…so I can bust yo ass." Apparently, she knew this SS poseur from an earlier class. They talked and completely ignored me. I decided to leave and check out the gym. I could hear yelling through the glass window and walls; it sounded like either a basketball or volleyball game.

Sneakers squeaked as kids shouted, "Pass the ball!" and "Over here!" There were six half-court games going on at the same time. Three on three; the boys played while the girls watched.

Three of the six games were grade twelves, two looked like grade elevens playing, and the last group was a mix of eights and nines. None of them good. A lot of air balls and lousy lay-ups.

I played basketball all through elementary school. I played in the morning, at lunch, after school, in tournaments, summer camps and clinics. So, I knew I could hold my own on the court. Even though I was four-foot-ten, barely a hundred pounds, I could shoot threes like a motherfucker and dribble around you all day. (Soccer was my primary passion, though; it was in my blood; my first love. Evenings and weekends during the spring season, all summer, and early fall, were dedicated to the soccer pitch.)

"Ahhh! Fuck! Fuck!" an eighter screamed. "Fuck! Ahhh, shit!" He had twisted his ankle bad. He held his leg and rocked back and forth on the ground. A few friends picked him up, walked him over to a bench near me, and asked him if he needed to see the nurse. "I dunno, fuck!" was all he said. He was just about ready to cry. He ducked his head down into his lap and shook. Broken, I thought. They got him back up, put one of his arms around each of their necks, and helped him hobble out of the gym.

"Hey, you," I heard a voice call. "You play?" This kid who looked Japanese or Korean or maybe Chinese—I couldn't tell—was pointing at me. "Come on." He motioned for another kid to join him, completing the three required to play.

Then there was some shuffling from the other team. They were talking with a kid who had a bandanna and matching Air Jordan shorts on. He looked serious when he walked on the court, swaggering and high-fiving his team and—fucking fuck!—my bus stop nemesis: Michael Underwood.

Fuck me.

He came right up close: "It's my bus"—he pointed to the floor—"and my fucking court."

I swallowed hard and deep. Was this guy for real? The silence assured me so.

"We get first ball," my teammate said. He was a lanky kid who wore glasses that were strapped to his head.

I didn't want to play anymore. I wanted to get the hell out of there—fast. But suddenly I found myself holding the ball, dribbling around my two opponents, and taking a shot around the free-throw line. Nothing but net.

"First to ten wins," my other teammate said, indicating we would be playing one-point baskets unless a shot was scored from behind the three-point line, which would be two points. He was Jamaican. He wore a tucked-in yellow T-shirt with a big headshot of Bob Marley on it. His waist-high jeans were buckled tight and he had on black sneakers that looked like nurse's shoes. All soft soles with no pattern. K-mart special.

We scored.

They had possession.

Game on.

Underwood had the ball. He bounced left and right, dribbling around all of us. He did a three-sixty while moving the ball behind his back and around his body, finishing off with a superbly executed lay-up where the ball left the tips of his long black fingers and went through the orange hoop to swish white strings.

"Yeah—whatsup?!" he said, barbarically pounding his chest as he ran past me, celebrating the tie game.

1–1, our ball.

I faked a pass from the top of the key and took the two-point shot.

3–1, their ball.

Underwood dribbled, passed, his teammate scored.

3–2, our ball…

...it went on like this until the score was tied at 9–9 and it was our possession.

The bell rang but nobody stopped playing. I faked to my right and passed the ball behind me to my teammate and ran past Underwood, behind him and to his right. In that same swift motion, timing his assault perfectly, he spun one hundred eighty degrees and elbowed me with all his might in the face. My nose exploded like a red water balloon. Blood and snot poured out as I collapsed to the floor.

"Hey, man, what the fuck?" someone said.

"You got a problem?" Underwood answered.

Someone else said, "No, let's go, Tom."

Everything went black and sick and loud; my ears rang and I couldn't stand up.

"You forfeit, you lose." Underwood kicked me in the stomach and walked out of the gym, lost in the scurry of students.

I sat up and tilted my head back, cupping my hand under my nose. It was no use. I was spilling all over my shirt and floor and jeans. A fucking mess. And the last student who left the gym hit the lights, so it was pitch black.

I cried.

I cried hard.

My stomach clenched and flexed. I couldn't help it. I knew crying was probably the worst thing I could do, but it happened. And it wasn't because of the physical pain, no…not at all. That I could handle. Hell, my dad whooped me harder than this. One time, we were at this wedding, I was in, like, Grade 6 or 7, I can't remember, and he oversaw recording the whole thing on video. So, he connected the camera equipment to this super high-quality VCR system he bought, and he asked me to press REC when he signaled from his place near the front of the church. He didn't want to use the tape inside the camera because it was "poor quality." The one in the VCR was superior, from Germany or someplace. Anyhow, I was sitting at the table with the VCR, a sound mixing board, and some other gear I didn't understand. He gave me the thumbs up when the music began and he shot the ceremony, concentrating on getting all the right angles. At the end I pressed STOP and rewound the tape. Everyone left for the reception and he sat down at the table to play the tape…well, it was BLANK. He had the VCR connected to the video camera so he could watch it through the little eyepiece, but nothing showed up. He had this confused look on his face as he messed with the wires, thinking maybe he connected it wrong. He ejected the tape and went to the Sunday School room in the back of the church where he could use the TV and VCR combo.

Nothing.

Dead air. Black-and-white dots in a furious storm littered the screen. He swore in Romanian and came back to gather up all the equipment and pack it into the trunk of our Buick.

He never said a word. Never even looked at me. I sat in the front seat while he drove.

Then, about fifteen minutes into the drive to the reception hall, he back-fisted me with all the force he could muster, said I was "prost" (stupid), "mucos" (snotty), and a "dobitoc" (a dumb-ass, basically).

I bled.

I cried.

How would he look to his friends? With no memories of their wedding, they would shun him. He would be the laughing stock of the Romanian community.

And then it hit me: instead of pressing REC, I must have hit PLAY.

Oh, Jesus, fuck. Dad figured it out, too. There was no evidence of anything being recorded (one could tell by looking at the ribbon inside of the VHS tape). At first, he thought maybe he connected the shit wrong, but no, it was me.

My mom was home with my sister, so she did not witness any of this.

I bled some more…

The lights in the gym flickered back on and I had to squint; they already adjusted to the darkness and the depth of my thoughts. I lay there through the second bell, not moving. My nose finally stopped bleeding. I had my shirt pulled up around my face, soaking it all in. I didn't move.

Footsteps rushed to my side. "Hey, you okay?" I heard a male adult voice. He pulled the shirt down, revealing my face. "Don't move," he said, "I'll be right back."

* * *

Lip busted, nose swollen, black-eyed and sore, I walked to my P.E. class after the school nurse cleaned me up. She asked me if I wanted to go home. I told her that it was just a silly accident: I tripped and landed face first on the gym floor. She looked at me suspiciously, not really buying the whole ordeal. She didn't understand how my arms—a natural reflex—didn't spring out in front of me to stop my inevitable face plant.

"Three laps around the gym—let's go!" Mr. Anderson commanded. He looked at me. "You can sit this one out if you want, Champ."

"Thanks," I replied. "I'll just hang out on the bleachers." I held a big blue ice pack wrapped in a brown paper towel against the left side of my face.

"You know, if you want, you can go home. It's okay with me," he said.

"I'll wait for my friend to finish. I like to go home with her."

He put his left hand on my shoulder, bent down, and spoke softly. "I know what really happened. A couple guys on my wrestling team saw the whole thing. And I am going to deal with this. I promise."

"Please, Mr. Anderson, it's fine, don't do anything. It was an accident." I didn't want this escalating. Just leave it alone…

He stood straight and tall. He had short gray hair on the side and was bald on top; his arms were solid, hairy, and muscular under a *Wildcats!* tee. He had a bit of a weekend warrior beer gut that extended past his barrel chest, but it wasn't enough to stop him from putting the beating to any man if the need arose.

"Let me tell you something," he began. "If you let this go on, it'll only get worse. Stop it now. Early. Before it gets out of control. That's why we're here. Teachers are your best defense."

"We're done, Mr. Anderson," a sweaty, salty-lipped girl said. "Now what?"

"Everyone line up against the far wall," he yelled over the top of her head.

When the final bell rang, I gathered my stuff from my locker and closed it for the day. I sat on the main hallway steps near the office and saw Michael Underwood's face staring back at me through the window. He was seated, alone, and waiting for someone. Then I saw Mr. Price, our principal, call him to his office. Underwood looked back at me and made a cutting motion over his neck. His malicious grin exposed ivory fangs that would love to sink themselves into my weakened flesh.

I returned the smile with a bold middle finger and lipped the words "Fuck you."

"You sure you wanna piece of that?"

I turned and saw Robert Cook and Jeremy Freemont standing two stairs above me, watching the whole scenario unfold.

"No, he doesn't. But if you don't fuck off, I'll crush your other nut," Alex said. She came out of nowhere, holding a massive math textbook with both hands, as if to strike.

Cook actually (and probably subconsciously) covered his crotch area with both hands, like soccer players do when forming a wall against a free kick.

"When you gonna fight your own battles, Blossom?" Jeremy said as he and Robert walked out the front doors.

"You know, you really gotta let me get in a word or two with those guys," I said. I was a little miffed that she always seemed to come to the rescue. I loved her for it, but I needed to take care of some things on my own.

She came in close, lips right next to my ear, and whispered, "Your breath really stinks."

We both laughed heartily and hugged each other. I didn't care who saw. I could only see out of one eye anyway, and that one was staring at my best friend's pretty little face as she let go and said, "All right, Blossom, let's go catch a bus."

*   *   *

About a week passed without any *interaction* from Jeremy, Robert, or Michael.

And it felt good.

I felt good.

It was another sunny Wednesday afternoon and I was at my favourite place in the world: the soccer pitch. My nose itched, and I sneezed every couple of minutes because the custodian had just cut the lawn. But I was ready. Allergies or not, this try out would be a walk in the park.

Alex was reading a book on the concrete bleachers. As I looked in her direction she gave me the thumbs up and a smile. The breeze played with her hair; she squinted and blocked the sun with a hand on her forehead in a sort of crooked salute. She wore mid-thigh purple shorts with a white top; she rubbed her legs every so often and the sun kissed the whiteness of her calves. She took off her socks and sneakers and wiggled her toes as she dived back into her novel.

I was pretty much the only person on the playing field. The assistant coach, Brad something-or-other, was strategically placing cones around the turf and checking his clipboard every few minutes to ensure he was setting it up right.

More potential players started showing up. I said "Hi" to a few of the guys I knew and a few others that nodded in my direction. The coach—a tall, Italian-looking fella with shoulder length, raven black hair, whose name I never caught—finally showed up. He handed out red and yellow tank-top jerseys with numbers on the back. His assistant came around with his whistle and big clipboard to ask our names. He wrote them down next to the corresponding jersey number and what position we wanted to play. Coach then made us run a few laps to warm up and split us into two teams. We ran through some ball drills—shooting, dribbling around cones, passing, corner kicks to players that would head the ball into the net, and so forth. After about forty-five minutes, we played a full-field game to get an idea of who's who and assess our game-time skill levels. Brad gathered up the cones while Coach Rocca—I finally caught his name when another student called to him—split the teams and assigned positions.

"Okay, guys," Coach Rocca shouted, hands cupped around his mouth, "forty-five minutes—let's see what you're made of!"

I was surprised at how poorly a lot of the students played. I mean, it looked like some of them have never even touched a soccer ball. And the ones that were good, never really had a chance to showcase their true skills because they were getting fouled by the inexperienced ones. I, on the other hand, found my way around quite easily…because of my size, and my speed, once I had the ball, you weren't getting the fucker. It belonged to me. I owned it. And I scored two goals to prove it.

I usually played midfield, but I ended up emulating both midfield and forward positions. Coach Rocca keenly watched as I ran up one side of the field and down the other; at times, I covered all necessary positions without breaking a sweat. My lungs expanded and took in air. I was in my element and no one could touch me on the soccer field. The game was a part of my DNA; I was born with it in my blood. It was excellence on a cellular level... since I could walk I had been kicking a ball and playing on city teams, schools, and youth leagues.

"Five minutes—push hard! Come on!" Rocca announced.

Yellow jerseys—us, me—were up and winning 4–2.

I dribbled near the top of the penalty area and passed to one of my teammates. He took the shot and it soared over the net. I swore. But I didn't really care. I knew I had made it. Then I looked toward the bleachers and she was gone...

Her backpack and novel were there, but no Alex.

Coach called us in with the final whistle.

"All right, boys," he said, "everyone did well,"—bullshit—"but as you know, we have to pick and choose. And some of you won't make the cut. I can only keep eighteen players and there's about thirty here. So, Coach Brad and I will discuss the picks later tonight and post our selections tomorrow on the outside gym wall. Any questions?"

"If we get cut this year, can we still try out next season?" a boy to my left asked. Blind paraplegics have more athletic prowess than this mess.

"Yeah, of course," Coach Rocca replied. "You can *try* as many times as you like." He gave they young lad a placating smile, knowing full well there wasn't a chance in hell he'd ever see an actual game.

I saw Alex up on the grassy hill next to the bleachers. She was getting chummy with that goth dude she'd been talking to every so often in the hallway. They were passing a cigarette back and forth and taking deep long swigs from his bottle of Coca-Cola. Somehow, though, I knew it had more than just carbonated food colouring and caramel inside. It was how she would take a swallow and then shake her head from side to side, smacking and licking her lips and giggling. She looked girly, not like I was used to. It was like the maturity fell off her and she was covered in this childish vapour.

"Leuca, right?" Coach Rocca pronounced my last name perfectly.

"Uh, yeah, that's me," I said, distracted. I looked him in the face, turning my attention away from Alex and her weirdness.

"Cristiano, that's a good Italian name," Rocca went on.

"I'm Romanian, actually. And my friends call me Cris."

"Well, Cris, I think you've got a bright future here. You play exceptionally well. And I think it's obvious you made the team. But, I'd like to ask: how would you feel about trying out for the grade eleven squad?"

"You mean right now?" I was—and sounded—confused.

"No, not now, tomorrow."

I paused. "Uh, yeah, I guess."

"Think about it tonight, okay? You can let me know tomorrow. There's no pressure. I just think you'd be the perfect addition."

That was the nicest thing anyone had said to me in a long time, maybe even ever.

"Okay, I'll see you tomorrow." He nodded and turned to Brad and started going over the Grade 8 roster.

I walked toward Alex, who was still flirting with the guy but now they were lying down on the grass, looking up at the sky, and talking about government conspiracies and highly intelligent beings from other planets that probably already live among us.

"Hey," I said. "I'm gonna go change. We catchin' the bus together?"

She sat up on her elbows—goth guy remained still, laid back—and said, a little slurry, "Wecatchabus, yeah. Immahere."

"You all right, Al?" I said, concerned.

"He calls me *Al*," she said to goth boy, who was out cold.

I bent down next to her. "Hey, let's…let's go." She reeked of alcohol and pot; her eyes were a little glassy and she was looking right through me.

"Where?" She shrugged her shoulders. "I like it right here, next to—what was your name?" She shook the passed-out piece of human flesh next to her, but received no response. "I can't remember his name. Jesse? Jamie? Jack? Ha, ha! No, not Jack. He's not a Jack—"

"Look, I gotta get changed. I'll come back and get you in a bit, okay?"

She gave me a goofy smile and mock waved. Whatever she smoked, drank, or ingested was now taking full effect…

The boys' locker room was underneath the gymnasium in a subterranean creation. I walked down two short flights of stairs to enter. It always smelled raw, wet, and grassy, like the forest after a rainstorm.

The concrete walls looked as though they were bleeding water with beads of moisture dripping everywhere. A little steam was left over from the last few students who used the showers. And now it was my turn.

I opened my big blue locker, almost forgetting the combination, removed my backpack, and pulled out my Levi's and a T-shirt with Yoda on the front, and a fresh pair of socks. I quickly got out of my sweaty, stinky, soccer gear and headed for the showers.

I hung my towel on the outside hook and closed the curtain in the one-man shower stall. I was happy that BCSS had single stalls; I couldn't have done the group thing, even though I was alone right now. I turned on the hot water. It was just barely lukewarm after everyone else had already used it. But I wouldn't take too long, a quick scrub—with the little soap bar I carried in a plastic case—rinse, and off and running I went.

As I lathered myself up, I thought about how cool it was that Coach Rocca wanted me on the eleven team. I'd surely be playing senior ball within the next two years, which could secure a scholarship to either Simon Fraser University or the University of British Columbia.

I dropped the soap, and when I went to pick it up, I thought I heard voices. I opened the curtain and poked my head through, but, because the showers were around a tiled corner in their own little alcove, I couldn't see into the locker area. I quickly finished rinsing—still full of energy, as if I didn't even play a sport for the past two hours—and then turned the water off. I reached my hand through the curtain and looked for the towel that hung on the hook.

Fuck.

I poked my head through.

Nothing—it was gone!

What?!

My heart rate immediately increased, pounding and thumping in my chest, as I began to panic. I was close to hyperventilating. I got dizzy and nauseous. I knew exactly what this meant.

I stuck my head back out, looked around, didn't hear or see anything. I tiptoed toward my locker, covering my penis and testicles with both hands, shivering, cold, dripping.

Every kid's worst nightmare unfolded before me: all my belongings were GONE.

My backpack: GONE. My clothes I left on the bench: GONE. My everything: totally and completely GONE.

"Hey, look at Blossom, all naked and clean," Jeremy Freemont said sauntering down the stairs. He stood in between Cook and Underwood.

"Fuck you—where are my clothes?!" I yelled, almost crying, my voice crackling with terror.

"Fuck me? Looks like you're the one that's fucked, shitbag." Freemont gave me the finger and ran back up the stairs to the gym, followed by Cook and Underwood.

I heard the outer door slam shut. Anxiety tremors seared through my entire being.

"WHY WON'T YOU LEAVE ME ALONE?!!!" I screamed at the very peak of my lungs. My throat burned. I could taste blood as my stomach heaved from the pressure I released.

Now what? I was stuck. I paced frantically around the benches in the locker room, shouting toward the top of the stairs, "Hey, anybody up there?! Hello?!"

Zilch. They were gone like yesterday's news.

I looked around for anything I could use to cover myself and head back upstairs. But there was absolutely nothing. Except for…

…the shower curtain. I tugged on it until I almost snapped the rod it hung from. The circular metal rings that held it together were impossible to tear. That sucker was staying exactly where it was. And so was I, for the time being. All I could do was open each locker, hoping and praying that someone left something behind I could use to at least get up to the main floor and either call Alex or call my mom to bring me some clothes. What the fuck would I say to her? "Hey, Mom, I'm at school, naked and cold, can you bring me something to wear? Thanks. See you in a bit."

I had no choice. I had to try to get upstairs and shout from there. I slowly opened the door at the top and looked around. The gym lights were off and nobody was in sight. I heard some whistling in the hallway and then singing in, I think, Spanish. Probably the school janitor, I thought. I was a little more hopeful now. My heart still hammering in my chest and now it felt as though it was climbing up my throat.

Fuck it. I took the chance and ran across the gym floor, on the balls of my feet, cupping my front and shaking uncontrollably. When I got to the far doors that lead to the rest of the school, I saw the janitor mopping the floor near the entrance. He had on a cassette Walkman and was whistling and repeating the word "bamboleo" over and over again.

"Hey—hey! Yo—help!" I yelled in his direction.

Nope.

"Yo—hey!"

Not a chance. The man was lost in a South American trance.

I pinched myself hard, thinking this could not possibly be real. There was no way this was happening. I wasn't naked in my high school gym. I was not crying right now, shaking and shivering and sitting against the door with my ass crack on the cold floor. This wasn't happening. Couldn't be.

Suddenly, the door to my left opened and an angel appeared out of nowhere.

My guardian angel—Alex.

She snapped on the lights and looked around, and didn't even notice me sitting on the floor, a foot and a half from her. She just kept on walking toward the boys' locker room, swaying and sashaying like a drunken wench.

Then, because Alex is Alex, she turned around and looked right at me. "I thought I smelled wet balls. What the hellareyadoing?" she said. She couldn't find a proper speech rhythm. "Youfeelingallright?"

"Alex," I said standing up and forgetting to cover myself. She laughed and I was glad she was stoned and a little tipsy; maybe she wouldn't remember this. "I need you to get me some clothes, fast." I was holding her by her arms, both elbows in my hands. I was so nervous and cold my penis was pretty much completely inside me.

"Um, why are totallynaked?" she asked.

"Never mind that. Just go to the Lost and Found and find me something."

"Where's at?"

"I don't' know! Ask the janitor outside." I took my hands off her and covered myself again, shoulders hunched over, still trembling. "Hurry! I wanna get outta here."

"Okay, but you promise to tell me everything?" She gave a snort and a giggle. My drunk and stoned Alex. Her parents probably wouldn't even notice or give a shit. Probably already inebriated at this hour, too.

She left through the double gym doors and went down the steps to the main hallway that led to the school offices. The janitor was gone. She turned the corner and was out of my line of sight. I closed the gym doors, walked over to the stage, hopped up on it, and wrapped myself in the red velvet curtain and waited.

The lights were on in the office, so that was a good start. Alex looked around but couldn't find the Lost and Found.

"Hey, what you doing here?" the janitor asked in his heavy accent.

Alex turned around, smiled, all teeth, and replied, "Um…I lost something. I'm…I just want the Lost and Found, okay?" She wasn't feeling well. She hadn't eaten enough today and now she was nauseous and dizzy. It was an excellent combination if you want to induce projectile vomiting.

"You hap to go now—"

"I just need someclothes—" Her belly heaved. Her face exploded, and her mouth launched forth a stream of bile and alcohol. It just missed Mr. Janitor; instead, the regurgitated blend landed on a nearby printer, soaking the paper and the buttons.

"Look what you done!" Mr. Janitor shouted. "Now what I do?! Chinga tu madre!"

Alex saw the photocopying room was open, and inside, near the back, there were little cubby-holes that held a few items of clothing. She found two hats, a pair of shoes, a couple of T-shirts, and an old pair of light brown corduroys.

"Hey—getta fuck out! Or I call police!" the janitor yelled.

Alex looked him straight in the eye. His cheeks were puffed out, his moustache sweating. She mustered all the strength she could and said, "Chill the fuck out, man. I just need to get some clothes and I'm outta here." This girl had more guts than a butcher shop.

"You a crazy puta…" He grabbed a rag from his pocket and started wiping the printer.

Alex moved quickly, feeling better now that she discarded the contents of her stomach. The nausea was gone, and she could see a little clearer. She grabbed the corduroys, snatched the first white T-shirt she saw, and yanked the only pair of shoes off the shelf. "Thanks," she said, running past Mr. Janitor.

"Ya, fuck, go," he said, mumbling some more in Spanish and mock spitting in her direction.

"Here—this is all I could find," Alex said, dropping the clothes on the wooden floor next to me.

I looked at the pants: they were a size 32. I was a 28. But I had to make it work. I slipped them on while Alex turned around and walked to the backstage area. She looked a little better now, not stumbling as much. The shoes were a size 11. I wore size 7. Again, I had to make it work. The T-shirt, though, brought the whole ensemble together: it was bright white with a picture of a rainbow hovering over a kitty cat. It read: You Are My Sunshine underneath its happy paws.

"How do I look?" I asked Alex.

She handed me a long piece of string. "For your pants," she said. "And you look like you have Tourette's syndrome and really bad breath."

I looped the string through my pants and tied it up at the front. They were all bunched up, but they'd stay up. I flopped around the stage in my clown shoes and hideous T-shirt. "They took everything," I said to Alex. "My clothes, my books, my bus pass. How the fuck am I supposed to get home? I can't call my mom."

"I'll call mine. It's all good," Alex said. "It's all good…"

*　　*　　*

I had enough money saved to buy another bus pass, pay for the two new textbooks, and buy the three novels I borrowed from the library. So, I had everything back but my dignity. Word spread quickly about what happened: Jeremy, Michael, and Robert spared no shame in sharing the details of my unfortunate incident with all who would listen. I never spoke a word of it and somehow it never got back to any teachers. Even if they did hear, most wouldn't want to get involved. They had their own world of work and home and groceries and taxes and 1200 students to deal with. Plus, there were yearly evaluations by the school board and parent teacher conferences, meetings, tutoring, meetings, and then some more meetings. There were husbands who cheated, mortgages due, and bills that needed to get paid. The last thing on their mind was some newbie Grade 8 who supposedly had to borrow a few clothing items from the Lost and Found because someone else took his *by accident*. That's the story they wanted to hear, anyway. The truth was something *they* would have to deal with but the lie could be left alone.

CHRIS PONICI

And so, the weeks went by and nothing of consequence happened. The janitor cleaned up Alex's mess and kept his mouth shut; he knew Alex could make up some lie about him giving her booze and trying to…well, you know. Given his history and two reprimands for drinking on the job, it would be a third strike. I decided against trying out for the Grade 11 soccer team—much to Coach Rocca's dismay—because I just wasn't in the mood or the right mindset, so to speak. And after I saw the squad, I was pleased at my decision: they were massive. I would have been tripped and pushed and trampled and crushed. But Coach Rocca knew something was going on and he kept a close eye on me. I started showing up late for practice and even missed a couple of games. I was still getting teased and Blossomed to death in the hallways, and now the moniker had devolved to "Blow Job Blossom." Not sure why, exactly, but it did.

"You excited about the field trip tomorrow?" Alex sat across from me in the cafeteria. Kids where shouting and laughing. It was a plethora of eights and nines and tens and elevens and twelves and teachers and insanity. "Blair and I are gonna get stoned and sit in the sauna."

Blair was Alex's goth friend. She was the only other person Alex really hung out with other than me. She hated girls and they hated her back.

"No, not really," I replied. "I think I'm allergic to chlorine. Every time I go I get all red and itchy and I can't sleep that night."

"Then don't go in. Get high and hot with us."

Grades eight through ten were going on this pre-Christmas-vacation field trip to the Burnaby Aquatic Centre, a newly renovated deal that made Canada Games Pool—with its indoor water slide and massive workout centre—pale in comparison. It was a yearly tradition before the winter and summer holidays to take a field trip together. Usually they went to the aquatic centre in the winter and the Vancouver Aquarium or the Langley Zoo in June, right before exams.

I'd never been high, nor did I want to be. This was especially true if I would have to sit in a hellishly hot and humid wooden sauna that would definitely make me sick.

"I'm just glad it's Friday tomorrow…and we get a couple weeks off," I said. "I've had enough of this shitty place."

Alex looked at me—my head hung low, chin to chest—and said: "Hey, it'll get better."

A BULLIED REUNION

* * *

The moon that stamped the sky on this dark and cloudless morning was brilliantly intense and clear. It hovered over the school parking lot like a spotlight shining down on the immaculate stage we call life; I felt cheery and upbeat.

I was the only one there, waiting for the others to arrive. I was anxious to get on with this swimming pool day and return home where video game vixens and sci-fi soldiers awaited my every command. It was where I could be safe and comfortable for the next two weeks. My life would soon be filled with sugar cookies and cakes and presents and fun. My dad would be intoxicated for the entirety of the holiday season and finally give me a wide berth and reprieve from his constant badgering about my marks and homework (even though I had yet to show him a B in any subject; I'd earned straight As all semester) and how I "have to go to medical school and be a doctor, no other way."

I caught the early, early bus—the 6:02. We were supposed to leave at 7:00 and arrive right when the pool opened at 7:30. My watch said it was 6:40 so I had a few minutes to walk around the track and stare up at the moon. I thought about scaling the big fence on the northern part of the field because the tall trees on the other side looked like they were hiding something behind their thick branches. So, with my backpack secured tight, I grabbed on to the fence and began my ascent.

It took me less than a minute to reach the top.

DEATH.

It was the biggest graveyard I had ever seen. The moon's eerie light shone upon the gravestones and a carpet-like fog floated inches above the dewy grass. I accepted the quiet stillness as a welcome friend, something to rely on. Something I'd like in my life. The nothingness of the moment. The singular understanding that no matter how good or bad or indifferent our lives were, we would all end up in a silent grave.

And there I was: thirty or so feet up, peering into a field filled with death, yet really looking within. I examined my own displeasure with how my life was progressing and how badly I wanted to see Michael, Robert, and Jeremy six feet under—soundless and mute. Hushed for all eternity...

The school buses roared into the parking lot at 6:50 sharp, followed by parents dropping off their kids. Soon the lot was filled with noise.

I was still on the fence, far enough away that nobody could see. I thought about hanging here until they left. Skip the whole fucking day. Climb over the other side and sit with The Silent. The Dead. The Gone. But I promised Alex I wouldn't ditch. And my mom washed my shorts and packed my bag with a couple of extra snacks. It'll be fun. I mean, it's an aquatic centre. Those bastards wouldn't dare try anything.

*   *   *

Terror seized and clutched my throat, cutting off the air supply to my brain. I thought I would pass out. A black curtain went down over my eyelids. The dreadfulness of what was in my backpack was too much. This, quite possibly, could send me over the edge.

I pulled out a pair of pink, tight spandex shorts from my backpack as I sat on a wooden bench inside the cold, damp change room. These were bike riding shorts I used back when I was in elementary school and had little or no fashion sense. They were totally pink except for two black stripes down each side.

How the hell was I supposed to go out wearing these? And why the fuck would my mother think that these shorts were the best selection?

I had no choice. I could not stay here all day. I had to go out and participate.

But I had an idea. She also packed a massive beach towel and I could use it as a cover. I would wrap myself in it, around the waist, and head straight for the hot tub, where I would stay most of the day. Or, I could get out from time to time and play some ping pong while still covered up.

Foolish ideas.

Fuck.

I asked a couple of other guys in the room if they had an extra pair—they gave me a strange look that said *Are you out of your mind?*

Maybe sneaking out with Alex through one of the doors and getting high and then hanging out in the sauna might be the best solution.

I waited till everyone was gone and out of the room, then slipped into the skin-tight shorts. I stuffed my shoes and bag and clothes into the large blue locker, put a quarter in it, and retrieved the orange key and pinned it to the top right side of my shorts. They were snug and pulled my balls up back into me. My penis looked like mushroom.

Barefoot and semi-cold, I took a pre-shower, as required, and swiftly made my way to the main pool, where I jumped in before anybody could really get a good look at me.

I swam a few laps and allowed the ambient noise to camouflage my negative thoughts and fears. The place was massive: it had one Olympic-size pool, a hot tub on each end, two big blue water slides that twisted and turned and spun around and finally dropped you off in their own little body of water at the end of the chlorinated ride, and a weight room/fitness centre up top where those exercising could look right down at all the half-naked strangers.

Alex was sitting at the edge of the pool in a one-piece swimsuit, her legs swaying back and forth in the water. She signaled me closer and I swam over.

"We found a door near the back we can prop open," she whispered once I was close enough. Goth boy wasn't around.

I was a little out of breath from the four laps I swam. "Where's your friend?" I asked.

She leaned over closer to me, her breasts bulging through the top of her suit. "He's waiting for me by the door. We're gonna do a quick hit and then hang in the steam room. The sauna's too packed with a buncha fucking fat Hindus."

Kids where jumping in and out of the pool, leaping from all four levels of the diving platforms, screams and shouts echoing all around like orgiastic banshees.

"I don't know, Alex," I said, shaking my head. "I've never even tried pot. And I don't think this is the best place to start."

"Come on—just one puff and we'll head back. You've had breakfast, right?"

"Yeah, a muffin, why?"

"You'll be fine."

All things considered, I thought it might help me chill and relax. I've seen how Alex gets on the stuff and she seems mellowed-out. Maybe I wouldn't worry about my shorts that much.

"Okay, I'll follow you," I said, slipping out of the pool. I walked next to Alex with my tight pink bum and peanut penis.

"Nice shorts," she said. "Mom packed your bag, huh?"

"Yeah."

We walked toward the two blue waterslides near the back of the building where Blair and his skinny frame stood next to the emergency exit. He was wearing over-sized, gigantic shorts that hung just below his hips (I could see the top of his pubes) and went way past his knees, to calf level. "Hey, wussup?" he said as we approached.

"Nothin', man," I said, looking at how tall and gangly he was. The same height as Alex. He was dry as a bone, having opted out of the required pre-shower.

"We'll slip out here"—he said, gesturing toward the door that said EMERGENCY EXIT ONLY! ALARM WILL SOUND IF OPENED!—"I can prop it open with a rock or somethin'."

We were covered quite well behind the last part of one of the water slides, so nobody could really see us. I could have sat there the entire time without any bother. How was goth boy going to execute his plan if the door alarm—

Alex said, "Won't the alarm ring when we open it? It says right there—"

"It's all bullshit, man," Blair said. "There's no alarm. Look"—he pointed to the top of the door—"there's no cord or line going anywhere."

The guy knew his stuff.

"Okay, let's go," Alex said, nervously rubbing her hands in excitement.

Blair reached into one of his pockets and pulled out a small roach (I knew now why he decided to skip the pre-shower), just enough for one or two puffs each. He then pulled a roach clip from his other pocket and handed it to Alex, along with a tiny Bic lighter. "Here," he said, "hold these." And with a slight push the exit door opened, to no fanfare or sounds of whoop-whoop or anything other than the proverbial squeaking.

The cold rush of air that hit my chest felt as though someone threw a bucket of ice on me. I gave a quick shiver and stepped outside; Alex followed close behind as Blair jammed a rock in between the door and frame. Alex clipped the end of the roach to the small, tweezer-like tool that Blair gave her and lit it, took a big hit, and passed it to Blair who copied her flow. Then it came around to me. "Inhale that shit," Blair said—and I sucked it back the best I could and swallowed the smoke, exhaling soon after. I coughed.

Hard. And for a bit, I couldn't stop. "Good. Get that into your lungs," Blair coached. And then he and Alex took another hit before it died.

"Okay, I'm freezing, let's go back in," I said, trembling.

Alex opened the door and we followed her.

The sounds of life inside the aquatic centre seemed distant, like everything was farther away. I couldn't feel my feet, and my legs felt like a mixture of jello and rubber. "I think I need to sit down," I said to Alex. I could hear my voice inside my head but wasn't sure if Alex heard it or not. She acknowledged me with a smile and motioned to follow her.

I said I wanted to hang in the hot tub for a while, I was too cold to walk all the way around to the other side where the sauna and steam room were. Blair gave me thumbs up and walked away with Alex as I dipped my entire body into heaven. The heat instantly warmed my body. I fully submerged myself a couple of times to let my head and ears thaw out and then sat at the very far end, water up to my neck, and stared at nothing at all. The best part was that nobody seemed to notice my swimming ensemble. And even if they did, I didn't notice them noticing, so who gave a fuck? The goofy smile on my face said as much.

I tilted my head back, shut my eyes and rested the curvature of my neck on the edge. Students splashed around and raced from one pool to another. Lifeguards blew their whistles and shouted "Hey, get off there!" Those teachers that braved the event and changed into their swimsuits, talked and joked loudly a few feet from where I was. They referred back to their younger years of liberty and independence, when they themselves had the freedom to not have a care in the world… "When I was in high school…" and "My parents would have killed my sister and I if we [insert misbehaviour here]…" They seemed, as teens, to have had the same issues with parental authority and academic fears as those they now taught. But then why did most of them act as though they were never children themselves? Why did they speak to us as if *they* came out of the womb at thirty years of age?

…sharp pains in my lungs and chest. The clamour around became muffled and silent. My heart beat faster and louder and was about to explode and breathing became—couldn't breathe. Pushing and splashing and grabbing and holding and screaming—

"Come on, Cris," I heard someone say. My back was freezing. Cold and hard. My face slapped—once, twice, again. "Come on, Cris." Then—a kiss:

filled with air and the taste of cherries and life. Followed by a sudden eruption of water and undigested muffin. I was on my side, heaving and throwing up fluid like a loosened fire hydrant.

"There you go," the same person assured, "you're all right…"

When I opened my eyes, I was lying on my back again, staring up at the face of an angel. Cliché, I know…but it's the fucking truth. She had the most beautiful, calm and wonderfully bright smile. Her eyes were the color of an exotic sea. Her hair like Egyptian gold. Her voice was the sound silk would make if it could speak.

"Let's sit you up, come on," she said.

Silent and still students watched as my saviour pulled me up to a seated position, held my hand, and gently rubbed my back. Her eyes caressed me with kindness.

"Thanks," I said, embarrassed that I had somehow passed out and slipped under.

Then the giggles started. And then they turned into full blown laughter…

My guess is that when I was pulled up and out of the hot tub, my shorts caught a sharp edge of tile and tore open near the crotch, exposing my flaccid and small penis.

Petrified and cold, I sat motionless, my brain unable to process what to do next. As the laughter and pointing increased, and nobody was doing anything, IT happened: my dear saviour kept lightly rubbing my back with her right hand and then COVERED my privates with her left. I felt the soft warmth of her hand around my tiny testicles. She cupped me ever so softly and yelled, "Would somebody get him a towel!"

I sat in the lifeguards' office covered up in a Caribbean-print beach towel. Mr. Anderson, with his big bulky calves and naked belly, sat to my right as I filled out my name and address on a sheet attached to a wooden clipboard. A full report would be filed, including, I guessed, the questionable concealment technique used by the very dear lifeguard who breathed life back into me, and who now stood just a few feet away talking to one of her colleagues about the incident.

"I think I'm done," I said, humiliated. I handed the clipboard to Mr. Anderson.

She walked toward me. A cascade of loveliness. My stomach was hollow and I thought I might have to throw up again. I'd never felt attraction before. She had the longest, leanest legs I had ever set eyes on. Her bright red one-piece—like the ones those *Baywatch* babes wore—hugged her body beautifully and curved up around her waist, right above her hip bone, exposing gloriously formed outer thighs. Her rounded breasts jiggled and bounced with every step she took. As she sat down across from me in a plastic patio chair, I couldn't help but look down at her tightly wrapped and carefully concealed—

"So," she said, leaning over, elbows on top of knees, "how do you feel? Better?"

I cleared my throat nervously. "Yeah, I do, thanks."

She looked at Mr. Anderson—who was going over the details of the report—and then back to me and whispered, "They don't know about your little trip outside…" She touched her forefinger to her thumb, making a smoking gesture. She winked, then added, "Your secret's safe with me."

After changing back into my clothes, I sat in the bleachers above the Olympic pool reading an *X-Men* comic book I had in my bag. Given the circumstances, Mr. Anderson gave me the opportunity to go home if I wanted. He called my house, but nobody answered, and I didn't know my dad's work number off by heart. So, I had to stay for the rest of the day. I snuck down into the far corner, trying to make myself as invisible as possible. I wasn't allowed to sit out in the main entrance area. I had to be within "viewing distance," as Mr. Anderson so graciously put it. In the change room after, he commented about how lucky I was to get a hand job from the "hottest piece of ass" he'd ever seen. (I was a little surprised at his vulgarity, but being that we were alone, and I had no intention of creating any more problems [especially with the wrestling coach], I brushed it off. I didn't fully grasp the term "hand job," but imagined what it entailed from previous schoolyard discussions.)

And so, after the twelve o'clock break for lunch—where students congregated and ate around me on the bleachers, wrapped in towels and shivering and shouting and laughing and high on the life they lived—I decided, after working up the courage and confidence, to walk over and talk to my pool princess, who was once again sitting high up at her lifeguard post. Her legs were crossed. Her feet were a fetish delight with perfectly proportionate, delicate toes and just a hint of clear polish. Her ankles were thin and slender connecting to wonderfully toned calves.

"You've been eye-fucking her for, like, fifteen minutes," Alex, the ever-present narrator of my life, said. "Why dontcha just go to the bathroom and get it outta your system?"

"Shut up, will ya? I'm not lookin' at anything," I replied.

"Hey, I'm sorry," she said. "I know this probably sucks for you. Hangin' out after all that went down. Everyone seeing your junk and stuff."

I ignored her and took another quick peek around me. Everybody was in their own little world; nobody really cared anymore. Yeah, sure, I saw a few eyes and heard a couple of whispers here and there but, all in all, I was left alone. Since everyone seemed distracted with their lunches, and I was finished talking to Alex, I resolved once again to talk to—

But she was gone! Her post was empty and another blue-eyed blond—this one of the male variety—was climbing the small ladder to sit upon her throne.

Shit.

I felt a slap on the back of my head. "Well look who it is: pretty little petite penis," Michael Underwood said, quite poetically, I might add. Jeremy and Rob, the ever-present pillars in Michael's life, stood on either side of him.

"How clever," Alex, to my defense. "I hope you didn't strain your brain over that one."

"She's probably got more cock down there than you do, Blossom," Rob said.

I waited for Blair to rebut and verbally protect. But nothing. He looked away like a coward. *Some friend you have there, Alex.*

"And if I do," Alex started, "maybe you should *suck it*, asshole."

A collective "oooohhhh" from all three tyrants.

A shadow formed behind the group. "He's more of a man than any of you three will ever be." They all turned around at once and saw my ravishing rescuer standing tall and proud, arms crossed, pushing up gigantic amounts of cleavage and tapping her right foot. Her look said more than disapproval; it was almost disgust. "You three are done for the day." She pointed. "Go get changed," she said.

"Fuck this noise," and "Bullshit," and a sarcastic "See ya later, Blossom," trailed the three as they left.

"How are you feeling?" She squatted down in front of me. "You look a lot better."

"Pretty good, thanks," I replied. "Can't wait till the day's over. Been a crazy one."

"What's your name?" Alex asked, knowing I was way too shy.

"Miss Diamond. But you can call me Lena," she said, looking right at me.

Of course her last name was *Diamond*. It had to be. It was either that or Miss Sapphire or Miss Gold or Miss Pearl or Miss Precious or Miss—

"I'm actually trying to get on full-time at your school. I'm subbing at Burnaby North right now, and I'm here part-time." She was straddling the bleachers next to me now. Alex moved up one row to create a bit of distance. Miss Diamond—Lena—gave us her full attention and looked at us equally when speaking. The cadence in her voice made me feel all warm behind my ears. My head felt soft and light.

"That's cool," Alex said. "What do you teach?"

"Social Studies 10 and PE, once in a while. Mainly the gymnastic component. But that only lasts a couple of weeks."

I couldn't help but stare as she looked at Alex and answered all her questions about how old she was (28!), and why she got into teaching. It turns out she wanted to be an Olympic swimmer and then eventually coach at the highest level, but was involved in car accident and spent a month in the hospital. She missed a bunch of competitions and life passed her by. Her dad died, her mom was devastated, the whole gamut. There was a bunch of girly stuff that I wasn't paying attention to as well.

A loud whistle echoed throughout the centre. Lunch was over. Everybody back in the pool.

"Well, you two enjoy the rest of your day. And if I don't see you again before you leave, have a great Christmas, okay?" Miss Diamond said.

"Yeah, you too, thanks," I said.

With that she swung her leg over—I swear I could smell lilac in her hair as she brushed past me—and walked away. Her wiggle was hypnotic. Every deliberate step she took firmed up one side of her immaculate tush, creating a flawless break between thigh and bum.

"You need to seriously get a grip," Alex said. "You're totally trippin' over that."

"She's spectacular," I said, my eyes still fixed on her. I felt an instant transition into manhood. I went from 13 to 23 in 2.6 seconds.

Alex was back in the pool, splashing around with that bone-faced gothic weirdo who was really starting to get on my nerves. Michael, Rob, and Jeremy took turns doing flips off the high diving board. None of them were brave enough to jump from the highest platform. It was Olympic height and looked as though you could touch the ceiling when you were up there. I pretty much just sat in the same spot reading and watching and reading some more. I was fidgety and eager to get the fuck home.

The final whistle signalled that the bus would leave in fifteen minutes. "Let's go, come on! Everyone out!" Mr. Anderson was giving his lungs one final workout. He clapped his hands in rapid succession, curled his lips, and whistled on his own while shouting "Quick showers—quick change, let's go!" He slapped students on the back as they made their way into the change rooms.

I put my comic book into my backpack and pulled out my bulky, red Sony Walkman, slipped on the foamy headphones, and pressed PLAY. I cranked the volume to MAX and blasted track number nine on *Appetite for Destruction*. "Sweet Child O' Mine" was passionately fitting as I exited the swimming area and saw Miss Diamond behind the desk, booking swimming lessons on the phone and looking as busy as ever. When she saw me, she mouthed the word "wait" and raised a finger, indicating that she'd only be a minute. I was a little confused but sat down on one of the plastic chairs around a matching table with messy junk food and candy wrappers all over it. The main foyer was almost completely empty, except for a couple of older ladies who looked like they were waiting for some sort of senior citizen exercise class to start. They were wearing bright blue track suits and white (!) sweatbands wound tightly around their foreheads. Right when Axl was shrieking his loudest, Miss Diamond came out from behind the desk and sat next to me. She was wearing red shorts that came about three inches above her knees.

"Here," she said, handing me what looked like a laminated card of some sort.

"What's this?" I asked.

"It's good till December 31 of next year. You can come and go anytime you want. You can use the gym, the pool, anything." She reached across and put her hand on my knee, and then did a quick scan of the room. "You're very sweet. And I'm really sorry about what happened today. But as horrific as it was, it'll only make you stronger." She smiled.

It was a year-long pool pass with my name printed right on it. "Cool, thanks," was all I could think of saying. "I was actually thinking of maybe lifting some weights." *I was? When did this happen?* "Try to get a little bigger."

"Well," she replied, coming in closer, voice barely above a whisper, "I think you're the *perfect* size."

—A loud *bang!* was followed by a pack of lively students exiting the change rooms. Riotous laughter and brazen voices swore, shouted, and roared nonsense. Silly girls with wet towels still wrapped around their heads were slapped by horny boys.

Miss Diamond shot up out of her chair as if she were caught doing something bad and walked away without saying another word.

Alex was among the crowd. She came right at me.

"Slutty eyes over there," Alex pointed to my one true love, "she's trouble, man. I'm tellin' ya. She gives me the creeps. Adults aren't supposed to look at kids like that—"

"Well maybe she doesn't see me as a kid—I'm pretty fuckin' smart, you know?"

She stood over me. I wanted to get up, but she put her hand on my shoulder, keeping me fixed in my seat, and said, "Call it…a woman's intuition, or whatever. Just stay away from her. It's weird. That's all…"

Funny, if some older teacher that looked like John Stamos (her "total crush") gave her a little attention it would be okay. Just fine. But because it's me, it's "weird" all of a sudden.

"Come on, lover boy" Alex said, nodding toward the big yellow school bus.

*   *   *

My mom was passed out on the couch, again. TV on pretty much full blast. Some cooking show was just finishing up. My dad wasn't home yet. The message on the answering machine said he was going out with some colleagues for a drink. So, once again, it was just *me*.

I grabbed a can of Pepsi from the fridge, a bag of potato chips from the cupboard and headed down to my dungeon.

I threw my wet towel and shorts into the laundry basket outside my door, and placed the *Burnaby Aquatic Monthly Magazine* on my computer desk. After I changed into jogging pants and a *Simpsons* T-shirt—the one where Bart is racing on his skateboard and a talk bubble above his head says: "Don't have a cow, man!"—I laid on my bed and flipped through the magazine looking for the winter weight room schedule and pool hours during the holiday season. My query was clearly answered on page twelve: open every day from 7:00 a.m. till 9:00 p.m.—except Christmas and New Year's, with a half day on Christmas Eve. I kept paging through the small booklet, not really paying attention to anything, passing the time...until page twenty-three. There she was: Miss Lena Diamond in all her glory, standing next to her lifeguard post in her tight red swimsuit, smiling and holding on to the ladder that lead to the high seat. Her left foot was slightly arched, knee bent and leg turned inward, showing off a sharply defined thigh muscle. Her breasts were squished together showing cleavage, as always, ample and plump, nipples poking through.

Her picture was a part of a half-page bio that included a few lines about her teaching position at *Burnaby North Senior Secondary*.

I felt that hollow stirring again in the pit of my stomach. An exceptional nausea closed my throat. A full-blown erection poked against my loose joggers and my balls tingled, a painful pressure building inside them.

I locked my door. I took my shirt off and slipped out of my joggers, pulled a wad of tissues from the box that sat on top of my small Samsung television, and dove under my bed covers. It didn't take me long to find relief. I came while gazing into her eyes, which looked right at the camera and at me. It felt as if she was in the room. It was like her photo was alive and she knew what I was doing and was happy.

The phone next to my computer monitor called me out of my trance. It rang and rang until I finally got up. I quickly wiped myself and threw the crumpled, wet tissues into the bin under my desk.

"Hello?"

"You were jerkin' off, weren't you?" Alex said.

"No, I wasn't," I replied. "I was reading. What do you want?"

"Now I *know* I interrupted *something*—you're all pissy."

"You didn't interrupt anything."

"Oh, so you were done?"

"So what? It's not like you don't do it, Mrs. Stamos."

"Don't be talkin' 'bout John, now," Alex said, sarcastically; her voice mimicking a Southern drawl. Although I wasn't sure why...

"So whattup?" I asked.

"Just thought I'd check on my nearly dead and drowned friend, that's all," Alex said.

"I didn't nearly drown. I just got dizzy. It was no big deal. Everybody rushed in for nothing—"

"Cris—you were totally under the water. It was fucked up."

"Yeah, well, I told you I didn't wanna smoke up. It got me all sick. And it was just so hot. Ugh. Like, remember last year, when that Russian girl fainted in the steam room?"

"Yeah, that was crazy."

"Well, that's what pretty much what happened. I stayed too long in the hot tub. I looked like a dead prune when I got out."

"Yeah, all *shriveled* up."

"Fuck you, okay?" I didn't appreciate the vivid reminder.

"Come on, I'm just fuckin' with you."

I heard commotion upstairs. My mom was probably awake. The sound of numbers being pushed came through the line. I said, "Hello?! Mom?! I'm on the phone!"

"Oh, sorry," she said, her voice a home to a million frogs, and then hung up.

I listened for the *click* before I resumed. "I'm really not in the mood, Alex."

"Hey—we got two weeks off—everyone'll forget the whole thing by the time we're back," Alex said.

"Yeah, I guess..." I said, nonchalant.

"So...Miss Diamond...what'd she give you, anyway?"

I paused. Unsure of how to answer. I didn't want Alex to know any more than she needed to. I said, "Nothing, just a card to call in case I feel sick later." I heard her coughing on the other end. "You gettin' high again?"

"Yeah, so, what's it to ya?" she said.

"I just don't get how you think you're gonna be a cop with all that shit you smoke. I don't know too many pothead police officers. Do you?" I was glad to put the spotlight on her for a while.

"You know a lot of cops, do ya?" Alex—who should be a lawyer rather than join the force—always deflected questions, avoided direct answers, and rebutted, if possible.

"I'm just being a friend," I said. "I don't like it when my friends fuck up."

"So now I'm a fuck up?" she replied, her voice raising an octave.

"No. You know that's not what I meant. But that Blair dude…he's kinda not really with it. I don't know about him." I didn't hear anything on the other end of the line for a bit. "Alex? You there?"

It sounded like she hung up.

Shit.

I put the phone down on my end, rolled back onto my bed, and looked at Miss Diamond's picture for a bit. I wanted to touch her again, badly. I wanted to taste her lips, to feel her breasts against my chest as she breathed into me—

The phone! "Hello?" I picked up.

"Hey, sorry," said Alex, "my dad just got home—I had to get outta the kitchen. He smells like the pub again…anyway, I'm in my room now."

I took a long pause. I didn't want to upset Alex. She was really the only person in my life that I could talk to. The only one who understood everything about me.

"Hey, listen," I said, "I didn't mean that about Blair. He's all right, I guess. I'm just jealous when you hang out with him. I don't want anybody taking you away from me." Insecurity dripped over the line. My throat tightened.

"Awww…somebody got a crush on me?" I could tell by her baby voice mimicry that she had her lips curled in friendly mockery. "How sweet."

"I'm serious. I've got nobody. I haven't made one friend…and I don't think I will—"

"Fuck friends. You don't see me hangin' out at the mall every weekend, do ya?" She let out a "pffft" in a *who really gives a fuck* manner.

"Fuck friends! And fuck Rob and fuck Jeremy and fuck Michael!" I was unexpectedly furious now. The prospect of not having to deal with any physical or psychological suffering for the next two weeks brought a sense of satisfaction and relief, as well as outrage that I had to deal with these diametrically opposed emotions before the supposedly "most wonderful time of the year."

"Don't worry about those three; it's just a phase. They'll get bored and move on," Alex said. "Next year they'll find some other kid to pick on. It's the way the high school game is played."

"Yeah, great *game*. I wish I was on another team…" I said.

"You wanna catch a movie tomorrow? I think they're still playing *Terminator 2* at Metrotown."

Alex, as always, knew how to instantly cheer me up. "Yeah, sure. That'd be cool. I think I've seen it, like, five times."

"And that's on top of the three times you saw it with me, right?" Alex chuckled.

I smiled. "Yeah, that sounds about right."

"Hey, I gotta go—my dad's bangin' around upstairs and my mom just got home. I'll have to play referee for a bit."

"Cool."

"I'll meet you at the bus at noon, okay?"

I said goodbye and hung up the phone.

It then sounded like a rhinoceros smashed through our front door and began pounding and crashing and slamming into every wall and cabinet.

My dad was home.

*   *   *

Christmas and New Year's came and went in a flash. The two-week holiday felt like a long weekend rather than the much-needed reprieve from my hellish high school life. Mom walked around in her usual alcoholic stupor, with my dad not too far behind. He was also consuming his anti-anxiety meds like candy, trying his best to keep his frequent panic attacks at bay. Just before New Year's Eve, he had to buy some beer and wine for the yearly party we throw at our house—where my mom invites almost every single fucking Romanian we know within (what seems like) the entire province, jamming everyone together in our tiny little place—and he did not want to go out alone. He paced around the living room while I was watching television. He kept breathing in and out, in and out, exhaling harder with each breath.

"Cristian," he said, dropping the "o" from my name as he often did (my mom picked my first name, which, to be sure, has Italian roots, and my father could never quite decipher why she chose "Cristiano" instead of the Romanian version of "Cristian" [rumor was—among the catty Romanians that frequented our home—that she had a huge crush on some big time Italian actor when she was in university whose name was "Cristiano"; thus the origin]), "come with me."

The fear of driving alone when he was having an attack was bizarre and unreasonable. *What if I get into a car accident and nobody's there? What if I get lost? What if? What if...?* He went to work and back every day with no problem, but outside of his normal Monday to Friday, nine-to-five routine, he would clam-up and become this kitty cat unless he consumed copious amounts of alcohol (rendering him unable to drive) or popped a few pills (rendering him anti-social and numb). And so, after much prodding and promises of a McDonald's cheeseburger and fries, I relented and accompanied him to the liquor store so he could stock our shelves with beer and wine and vodka and rum. He was spending money he did not have to impress his friends.

So, except for going to the movies a couple of times—bus to Edmonds Station and then take the Skytrain to Metrotown Centre—I pretty much just laid around the house playing video games and reading. I finished *The Lord of the Rings* trilogy, devoured my comic book collection, and watched copious amounts of *Star Trek: The Next Generation, The Fresh Prince of Bel-Air,* and *Full House.*

But then the party was over, and it was back to school.

When I returned to class, it felt as though it was my first day all over again. Alex was sick and stayed home, so I was literally all *alone*. And with the semester switch-up in the next few weeks—all the teachers' focus was on final exams and how important it was to put our social lives on hold and concentrate on the tasks at hand—students were extra anti-social and stand-offish.

My first period class was French 8 and Ms. Lang was being unusually bitchy.

"I will fail all of you if you don't get at least 85% on the final exam," she said. We all looked at each other, not sure what to make of it. "It's worth 20% of your grade. And so far, YOU are my worst class. There are only two students over 85% and four between 67 and 73. That's unacceptable." She wore all pink again today: some sort of flippy-floppy, long-sleeved silk thing that came down past her waist with matching pants. Her shoes, two-inch heels, were white, and looked like something my grandmother would wear to a wedding or at Easter. "And—to the shame of all of you, we have three students failing. Although"—she shook her head and pursed her lips in frustration—"it's nobody's fault except their own. You know who you are." She looked directly at Michael, Rob, and Jeremy.

They snickered in unison.

"You think this is funny? This is your life!" Ms. Lang shouted. She actually shouted loud enough for, I am sure, the entire third floor to hear. "What will your parents think? Huh? What will the principal think of my teaching abilities? I have never"—she walked up the row toward The Trio and stood a couple of feet away—"had ANYBODY fail my class. Do you understand?"

No one blinked or took a breath. We waited for the volcano to cool down.

"So, you three will visit this classroom from three to four o'clock every single day until you're ready for the exam and you pass. Do you hear me?"

I felt this conversation would be better suited to have in private, not in front of 30 other students who were still on a Christmas high and wanted to ease back into the swing of things.

"DO. YOU. HEAR ME?" I thought Ms. Lang's forehead was about to explode. Her ears were pulsating, and her hands were actually *shaking*.

All three nodded.

"Good," she said. And with that, she returned to the chalkboard, wiped it clean, and began the lesson on conjugating verbs.

I called Alex at lunch from a payphone in the lobby.

"I've been fucking puking my face off all morning," she said.

"Maybe you're pregnant," I joked.

She did not laugh.

A pause. Then: "So, how's the first day?" she asked.

"It's all right. Ms. Lang went off on The Three Amigos. They're all failing."

"Good. Fuck those bros."

She always sounded so hip and cool. Like she was writing the book on being germane and in vogue.

"Anyway, I just thought I check on you," I said.

"That's sweet, thanks," she said. "I wanna tell you something, but not over the phone. Can you stop by after school?"

"Yeah, sure. Everything okay?"

"I'll tell you later. I'm not feeling well—I gotta run—"

The phone went dead. No dial tone, like in the movies, just dead air.

There was fifteen minutes left until the bell rang and lunch would be over. So, I thought I would go up to Ms. Lang's class and ask her a question about today's lesson. I wanted to ACE the exam, ensuring a straight "A" report card and the rewards that come with it: my dad promised me $20 per "A"! It would be an easy eighty bucks!

I reached the top of the stairs, made my way to the class door, and began to turn the knob. It was locked. I got up on my tippy-toes to see into the small window opening on the door. It didn't look like anybody was inside—

Then I heard the door unlock and open...

"The fuck you want, Blossom?"

It was Jeremy Freemont. He was holding the door with one hand and curling a fist next to his side with the other.

"Nothing," I said, barely audible. It came out as "nuh-ting."

I peeked around and saw Michael Underwood zipping up his jeans and laughing. When he came to the door he said, "You better get fuckin' lost, man." And then, "You never saw us."

They both brushed by me, giving me the evil *fucked-if-you-talk* eyes, and then disappeared down the steps.

The door was slightly open, so I thought I would look inside the class. It smelled like a homeless shelter: sweat and urine. Ms. Lang's purse was on her chair, open wide. My young imagination went wild and suddenly I knew what had happened—

"Well this is a nice surprise."

I froze. Ms. Lang walked into the room.

"Did you come to say hello?" she said.

"Uh..." I couldn't get the words out.

"What's that smell? Why is my purse on my chair?" She snapped her head around toward me. "Did you touch my purse?" she asked, puzzled. As her best student, this sort of behaviour would be out of the ordinary. "Oh, my, god…" She covered her mouth with both hands and stepped away from her purse.

"Ms. Lang, I just walked in the door and—"

"Who did this?" she asked.

I swallowed a rock. "I don't know. What is it?"

All she could do was point. I approached, cautiously, as if something would jump out and leach itself onto my face. I peered in…that wasn't soup floating around the bottom of her purse, soaking her wallet and keys and reading glasses and day timer and…

"Who did this?" she kept on. "You saw them; you *must* have."

"I swear—I just got here," I said.

"Get out! Get out!" Now I was being yelled at.

This wasn't going well, I thought. I had to do something.

"Ms. Lang, please, let me help. I can get some paper towels from the bathroom—"

"Just go away." She picked up her purse by the two straps—it was as big as a beach bag—and moved it to the floor. Nothing soaked through; it all sloshed up inside. There was nothing I could do or say, so I left. Just as I turned around, she said: "Go to the office, right now." Her expression advised me not to say another word; just follow orders.

I did.

* * *

The school office was quiet. The third period bell rang and so most teachers were in their classrooms teaching and inspiring—or, most likely, boring—their students.

"Come on in," Mr. Price, our principal, said. He sat down at his large wooden desk at the back of the main office. "Take a seat…"

There were two uncomfortable chairs facing his desk. They were made of solid wood and hurt your ass if you sat too long. I wiggled a couple of times to find my place and noticed that my hands were shaking a little and I found it hard to breathe. This was the first time I had EVER been in a principal's office under these circumstances.

"I am not accusing you of anything," he said, leaning back in his leather chair, eyes dead on me, both hands placed comfortably on the armrests, "*but*, another student saw you enter the classroom. And she"—he stumbled here, not wanting to reveal the tattler's identity—"—*they*, said you were in there for quite a while before Ms. Lang showed up."

"I was—I mean, not for long. I just wanted to ask her a—"

Mr. Price interrupted. "Look, Cristiano—can I just call you 'Cris'?" I nodded. "I know you didn't urinate in Ms. Lang's purse. I know that's not something you would ever do. But I *have* to punish someone. That's my job. So, you see, if I don't find out who did this, then I can only conclude, because of what a witness saw, that you were somehow involved. But—like I said—we both know that's not the truth. So…tell me who did it and we can get this over with."

There was no way in fucking hell I was going to rat on Michael or Jeremy. It would be social suicide. "Like I told Ms. Lang—I don't know. The classroom was empty when I walked in." I didn't say another word. I had just started watching a new show on television, *Law & Order*, and knew the less you say, the better. *Deny, deny, deny.*

He sat very still and said, "Come on, Cris, that's not the truth. You and I both know that."

"But it is," I said calmly. I was quite impressed at my composure. I gripped the sides of my seat as hard as I could to hide the shaking, but otherwise I was cool as a—

"Then I'm going to have no choice but to suspend you. And once I discuss the matter further with Ms. Lang, you may have to appear before the school board. You'd be facing expulsion."

It did not matter how hard I gripped my seat at this point, my chest—actually, pretty much my entire body—started shaking uncontrollably. I was cracking…

"It's up to you," Mr. Price said. He should have been a cop. He would have made detective in no time. "It's your call. You were in that classroom. And somebody has to take the fall. That's just the way it is…"

Well, then, it's shitty, I felt like saying. "But if I didn't do it—and you know that—how can you punish me?"

"Last chance, Cris. Who was in that classroom? I know you saw more than you're saying. I can tell. I've been in this racket long enough to know a hell of a lot more than any of my students. So, one more shot: who?"

The crossroads: spill my guts and face The Trio's wrath, or keep it shut and face expulsion and pretty much an end to my scholastic endeavors. Universities tend to frown upon this sort of thing; especially given the circumstances. I could see it now, in four years I would be in an interview pleading my case to the Director of Admissions at UBC: "I didn't piss in her purse. It was all a mistake. Please accept my application."

All I could say was: "If you really know a hell of a lot more than your students, then you *know* why I *can't* say anything."

I think he admired my courage. A corner of his mouth rose to a smile. He made this clicking sound and let out a deep breath. I could tell I stumped him. With all his years and all his experience, this was not a simple fix. He knew Ms. Lang's temperament. He knew she would take this right up the chain of command and demand justice. She would probably even sue the district. He knew that someone had to fry for this to appease the gods.

"You can go now," he said. And then went back to shuffling papers on his desk.

The room instantly got cold. I stopped shaking, though.

"What do you mean?" I asked.

"You've already told me who it was. You're free to go."

"But I never said anything." I was so fucking confused.

"Sure you did, just now. You told me you saw Michael Underwood urinating into Ms. Lang's purse. It's okay, I expected this. I have his elementary school file. And I knew he was a bad egg right from the start." He leaned over his desk, elbows on top, hands closed as if he were about to pray. "He was suspended four times in grade seven and twice in grade six. He spat into a teacher's coffee, he swore at Principal Winter, he—I think—even started a fire in the boys' bathroom."

"But Mr. Price—I never said anything. They'll know it was me," I said.

"Who's *they'll*?" he asked.

"They—them!" I said. "Michael and Jeremy and—" Shit!

"There you go: that wasn't so hard, was it?"

He tricked me. I lost.

"No," I began, "I—I didn't say anything." I fucked up.

"You can go back to your classes now," he said.

Fucking guy. I couldn't believe it. I got up to leave.

He looked at me one last time. "Everything'll be fine, you're in good hands."

Out in the empty hallway, I vomited into one of the plastic trash bins. And as I walked into my third period P.E. class, I heard the voice of Principal Price over the PA system. "Michael Underwood to the office, please. Michael Underwood to the office." This was unusual. Typically, the school secretary would call on students. Price must have been trying to send a message... but I wasn't sure to who—Michael or me...

＊　＊　＊

The next few weeks were the quietest I had experienced in my young high school life. Jeremy and Robert left me alone while Michael was gone. Word around school was that he only got suspended for three weeks (Principal Price said he wouldn't give up on him). And I heard from another one of his buddies that Price said he would break him in two if anything like that ever happened again. So, it was a welcome reprieve from the usual taunting and teasing. And Ms. Lang apologized for being "so rough" with me. She didn't have to but I appreciated the gesture. It didn't look like anyone knew about my *secret* meeting with Principal Price. Neither Jeremy nor Robert approached me, none of the students said anything through the grapevine, and even when Alex (whom I had told the whole story to) pressed her sources, she came up short. Nobody had a clue.

I knew Michael had his suspicions. I mean, who else saw him? I was the only person around. I had this self-doubt that plagued me throughout the day. It came in bursts. I was nice and calm, and then suddenly I felt this sense of impending doom and dread. It started at the top of my head and went to my stomach.

"You coming to the school dance tonight?" Alex asked, prodding me out of my thoughts.

"Yeah, I dunno…" I said.

"You look totally out of it," she said.

I shrugged my shoulders and put the rest of my books back into my locker. "Michael's back on Monday," I said.

The final bell had rung. It was Friday afternoon…

"So? Who gives a fuck?" Alex slammed her books into the locker. "Fuck him."

"Yeah, well, it's not that easy."

"Actually, it is, *Cristiano*," she mockingly said my name in her Hungarian accent. "You need to go to Principal Price and tell him you need some sort of"—her nose and lips twisted in a *Bewitched* sort of way as she looked for the right word—"protection."

"This isn't the mafia, it's high school."

"Coulda fooled me."

But she was right. I needed to do something to ensure that when Michael returned he knew it had nothing to do with me. I wasn't sure, though, that it would matter. He would still torment the hell out of me, no matter what he thought.

"I think you're right. I'm gonna talk to Price," I said.

"I'm tellin' ya," Alex said, "you gotta lock that shit up tight."

I gave Alex a frown and shook my head. "Sorry, I don't get your gangsta speak."

Alex stopped fiddling around with her locker and gave me a stare that would back off a bull. "Build a wall of people around you," she said. "One thick enough that even Michael can't get through."

*   *   *

School dances are not really my thing. I like the music and all, but I'm not big on the dancing part. I only went because Alex said I had to (she wanted an escape dance partner for when some creepy kid approached her). But so far things were going pretty well. The lights were dim, the music was blaring. The DJ—some Grade 11 kid that I have only seen a couple of times in the hallway—didn't really have sense of song order. (Color Me Badd's "I Wanna Sex You Up" was followed by Nirvana's "Smells Like Teen Spirit," for example.) I was hanging out in the corner, drinking 7-Up out of a big red plastic cup and chatting with the soccer team. We were 8-2 and crushing opponents. Basically, I was having a good time.

"Hey, you look like you're havin' fun!" Alex said, shouting over the music as students all around us were grinding to Tone-Loc's "Funky Cold Medina."

"It's all right," I said.

"You wanna get fucked?" Alex asked. She pointed to a blond girl near the exit doors.

"Uh…no, not really. Not here," I said, all weirded out by her comment.

"No, idiot, I mean—drunk! That chick over there's got some Bombay."

"Oh…nah, I'm cool. You go ahead."

"You sure?" Alex was right up in my ear now. Blondie looked our way and smiled a little. She looked to be in Grade 9 or 10. Alex noticed and jumped all over it. "You never know, maybe she'll suck your dick."

"You're a mess," I said, smirking.

Alex laughed, tossed her hair, and walked toward the blond girl. Fourteen pairs of eyes locked on to her ass like tractor beams in space movies.

"Man, she's cute." Devon was standing beside me. "Are you guys, like, going out or something?" he asked.

"No, just friends," I replied.

Devon played Right Forward on our soccer team. We never really spoke to each other off the field. Being that I played Right Midfield, he was on the receiving end of most of my passes, so we talked a lot on the pitch.

Thomas and Anthony, Centre Forward and Left Forward, came up to us. "Whattup?" Thomas said. He had the strangest looking skin I had ever seen on a person. It looked like he had a bunch of zits and popped them all at once, but the redness stayed. Like he was constantly blushing. "I heard Jodie's got some booze."

"She does," Anthony, wearing a buzz-cut, expensive black and red Air Jordans, a white Tommy Hilfiger top, and Guess jeans, chimed in. "She stole a whole bottle from her dad. She's gonna get totally hammered." The fucking kid dressed like a rap star that made millions a year. He even had this silver chain with a Mercedes symbol attached to it. Tacky, but kind of cool.

Thomas said: "I saw her sneak out back. I think that's where she's stashing the bottle. You guys in?"

Anthony and Devon didn't need much prodding. They immediately agreed and the three of them left without saying another word.

So, as usual, it was just me. Standing alone, sipping my almost empty cup of 7-Up, moving back and forth and tapping my foot to "Mama said Knock You Out" by LL Cool J and watching those around me laugh it up, smiling and high-fiving each other; even some of the teachers were mock dancing, acting like gangsta rappers and moving their arms in these cutting motions in front of their bodies, like they were the ones telling the story.

I turned toward the stage and I noticed that Rob and Jeremy were talking to the DJ. He had on a pair of big Sanyo headphones but only one speaker was over his ear, the other one was pushed upward near his temple as he listened to what Jeremy was saying. He nodded and gave Jeremy thumbs up, indicating, I guess, that he liked his song selection.

Jeremy bounced off the stage and, in perfect sync with "Gonna Make You Sweat" by C + C Music Factory, started dancing next to a little brunette.

He sucked. It looked like he had spiders crawling all over his back and he was trying to shake them off. He would do this jump/hop thing and then twist his body while dipping low to the ground. Nobody dared laugh because he could kick anyone's ass into next week. But it was glorious to see all the students, and even some teachers, turn around and snicker. Even I had a goofy smile on my face.

Rob noticed a couple of people laughing, and grabbed Jeremy by the arm. Jeremy pushed him away like he didn't care. He just wanted to hang out with—I think her name was Claire, or something—this brunette who had yet to move her body an inch. She stood there, watching this ridiculous dance show take place.

The pop was just about ready to go right through me. I could feel the pressure building. I had to piss. I threw my big red cup into the trash and headed for the exit. And as they closed behind me I could hear the start of EMF's "Unbelievable" pounding through the speakers.

Both the hallway and boys' bathroom were completely empty. The first of the ten stalls—I never use urinals—was full of shit and piss. It stunk like nobody's business. *Ugh.* I slammed the stall door shut, not bothering, or brave enough, to flush, and went and used the far one.

I closed the door behind me, unzipped my pants, and let 'er rip. I must have drank two litres of pop, because it was the longest stream I had ever had—

"—cause she's fuckin' hot, that's why!"

Two people entered the bathroom.

"Maybe if you could dance, you might have a chance."

It was Rob. Shit. And it sounded like he was talking to Jeremy. Okay, no worries…just stay put and don't move till they leave.

"*Dance* and *chance*…you be like a fuckin' poet," Jeremy said.

His words sounded a little slurred, and so did Rob's. They must have had a few sips of somethin'-somethin'.

"You wanna hoot?" Rob said. "I gotta couple hits left on this thing, then it's dead."

"Hold on," Jeremy said. He scanned for feet underneath the stalls. I anticipated it and quickly hopped up onto the toilet seat. *Phew*! He didn't see me. "Okay," he said, pushing himself back up to his feet, "let's do this."

"Wait—" Rob said. "Let's go into a stall—just in case somebody pops in.

"We're not hangin' out in a stall like a buncha fags," Jeremy said.

"What if a teacher walks in?"

Jeremy pondered the thought before agreeing. "You're right. Let's use the last one. It's right underneath the vent. It'll help kill the smell…"

"Yeah, if the shit stank ain't enough."

Then—the horrors of horrors: Jeremy pushed against my stall (I locked it shut), but it didn't budge. "What the fuck?" he said. And then bent down to check again. I held my breath. I saw his head poke out underneath the door. He was staring right up at me. "Get down and open this door," he said.

"Who is it?" Rob asked.

Jeremy slid back out from underneath the stall door and said, "Guess who?"

"Look, I don't want any trouble, guys," I stammered.

"There's no trouble," Jeremy said. "Just get the fuck out!"

Oh, boy…

Rob looked at Jeremy. "Cristiano?"

"Yup."

"Oh, goody," Rob said. He clapped his hands together.

I unlocked the stall, knowing it was the wrong thing to do, and opened it. They both stood, arms crossed, smiling, eyes a little bloodshot.

"How's it goin', buuudy?" Jeremy said.

The smell of shit was unbearable. That stall must have had ten pounds in it. I just wanted out. Fast.

Jeremy and Rob looked at each other. It was like they could read each other's minds. Rob quickly stomped over to the first stall—the source of the smell—and said "perfect" as he looked inside.

And then, without even having to say a word to each other, they tackled me to the ground, dragged me over to the first stall, and did the unthinkable…

"You put our boy in some deep shit," Jeremy said.

"And now it's your turn," Rob added.

I was as light as a feather. It took very little effort for them to pick me up by the legs and turn me upside down—each holding me by my upper thighs—over the toilet seat. It was effortless, really.

"Hey—stop! What the fuck!" I pleaded. "Put me down!"

"We will, don't worry," Jeremy said, snickering.

And with that—oh, yes, this is one for the books—they submerged my head in the toilet bowl. I tried to grab onto the rim and push up, but they pile-drived me with all their force into the feces-filled water.

My head was under for about thirty seconds. I held my breath but could feel water coming up through my nose and shit touching my face. I gagged and blew out over and over. They pulled me out and let go. I fell hard to the floor, twisted against the toilet bowl and stall wall.

"How's it feel, fucker?" Jeremy spat in my face.

I couldn't open my eyes. I could only imagine what I looked like.

They turned around and walked out of the stall. Rob said, "Keep your fuckin' mouth shut next time."

I heard the bathroom door slam shut. I slowly reached for the toilet paper roll near my head and tore off a good wad. I began to wipe my face and chin and neck. The shit was soft, like old stew, so it was all up in my hair. My white shirt looked like I threw up all over it. My jeans seemed okay and my runners were untouched. I kept tearing off chunks of paper and wiping myself furiously. Then I threw up. Mostly just pop and bile. The smell was horrendous. I flushed the toilet and left the stall.

The mirror said it all. I looked like *shit* (pun intended).

My face was red from all the wiping. I started to cry. Full-blown baby crying. Elbows on counter, hands over face. Snot dripping, balling my eyes out. Sniffling and choking, I fell to the ground and lay there on my back, completely defeated.

For the first time in my life I wanted to kill myself. I wanted to go home and swallow each and every last pill in the medicine cabinet. I wanted to lie down in the tub while it happened, naked and alone, shivering and cold as the permanence of it took effect.

I wanted to die.

I heard the door open and saw Coach Rocca. He bolted toward me. Leaning over me, he said, "Hey—you all right?" He put his hand on my forehead like he was checking me for a fever.

I slowly opened my eyes. Tears ran down the side of my face onto the tile floor. I barely managed to say, in a hoarse, defeated voice, "I'm fine. Just not feeling well..."

"What the hell happened? You're a mess."

I didn't respond.

"Here," he said, trying to get me to sit up, "let's get you on your feet."

I finally got up and leaned against the sink counter. I said, "Do you think you could take me home?" I was staring at the ground. I couldn't look him in the eye because I knew what he was seeing, and I respected him too much.

"Yeah, of course," he replied. "But first you need to tell me what happened—and no bullshit. Who did this? Was it—?"

"Please, Mr. Rocca, I just wanna go home..."

He didn't push the matter any further. He helped me get up and we slowly made our way down the hallway to the equipment room (or "The Crypt," as the jocks called it) in the school basement. He found an old Puma tracksuit that smelled like a mixture of rotten wood and wet dog. I put it on, threw my soiled clothes into a black trash bag, and discarded them.

We drove in silence the whole way home. When he pulled into the driveway, and I got out, he looked at me and said, "Hey, everything'll be fine"—*Where have I heard that before?*—and He walked me to the door.

I wanted to believe him, I really did. But I knew deep down that it was a falsification of reality. A total lie. These boys would never stop. I was weakness and they were strength. They were predator, I was prey.

It was almost ten o'clock. I was sitting on the edge of my bed. I was showered and clean, hair slicked back, with a fresh pair of pajamas my mom laid out for me. She spoke to Coach Rocca for a long while in our living room. (I never told him anything, but it did not take a genius to figure out what happened. He was once in high school, too, and could fill in the blanks of how I ended up looking the way I did.) She was angry and cried. I didn't hear any of the conversation.

"I want to meet with the principal on Monday," she said after Coach left.

"Just leave it alone," I said. "I can handle it myself."

Dad wasn't home and mom didn't know where he was. Earlier in the week he had talked about layoffs at work. Something about "downsizing" and "moving the company to Alberta." I wasn't really paying attention. He was probably out with friends tonight, drinking. The anodyne of alcohol eased his anxiety.

Mom was alone upstairs. She went from sympathy to anger in two seconds flat. How could I let them do this to me? Why didn't I stand up for myself? I should have run away and called for a teacher, blah, blah, blah.

"SHUT THE FUCK UP!" was what I wanted to yell at her. My brain was going a thousand miles an hour. I felt anger and confusion and remorse and fear and—for some reason, a strange sexual tension. My nuts hurt—I had a full-blown erection. My heart pumped violently. Blood flowed through every inch of my body. It was this visceral and primitive feeling of wanting to both kill and copulate at the same time. I felt like a raging animal; a jungle beast. My chest heaved up and down. I wanted to go back to that school and bash their fucking heads in with a baseball bat. To spill their blood all over the gym floor. To kill. To maim. To destroy those fucking brutes who took my innocence.

I wanted revenge.

CHAPTER 2:

Twenty Year High School Reunion (2017)

Time heals nothing, it only replaces memories.

It was seven o'clock and my Samsung lit up with a text. I had just walked through Burnaby Central Senior Secondary School's front doors for the first time in just a little over twenty years.

We are in this together. All the way... the next little yellow cloud bubble on my screen said. *We are gonna fuck shit up.* It was Alex.

I'm not sure if TELUS keeps track of everyone's texts on a database in a warehouse or office building somewhere. Because if they did, and Alex and I ever got caught for what we were about to do, writing *"we are gonna fuck shit up"* is as incriminating as it gets.

I tapped away on my screen: *Is the room ready?*

Does my pussy smell like flowers? Alex texted back.

I smiled as I walked toward the gymnasium. A woman talked loudly on a microphone and people shouted responses. A heavy bass beat wafted through the open doors as a couple of ex-students—one male, one female—stumbled out.

"Man, I remember when she'd get mad at us for wearing our hats in class," the guy said.

The girl, tipsy, holding on to his shoulder, said, "She was, like, this thin little thing and now she's all fat."

I wasn't sure which teacher was the target of their verbal assault. Nor did I really give a fuck.

"Excuse me," I said as I brushed by them.

"Hey," the guy said, looking at me, "You're—"

"Nobody," I replied, and gave him a look that said he should keep walking. It's not that I was more threatening now than back in high school. No, sir. I was five-foot-five and still weighed 135. But I had this *don't fuck with me* look that Alex said came with years of mental and physical abuse.

"It's 'cause you're a psychopath," she'd say when the look would suddenly appear.

"No," I would reply, "it's 'cause you're a cop and I'm not afraid anymore."

The gym smelled like sweat and perfume and stale socks. Up on stage, just like at every goddamn school dance, the DJ was spinning records—or playing CDs, whatever the hell they do up there. The alumni were bouncing around the floor to a hip-hop beat I did not recognize. (I preferred the classics these days. And by that, I mean Beethoven, Mozart, Vivaldi, and—yeah… you get it. [Alex would say to me that "all crazies like that violin shit"].) Directly across the room, opposite the large stage, I found the essence of this evening's purpose. It was the reason I made the trek on this cold winter night—just below zero outside, with a few flecks of snow landing silently on cars and walkways and rooftops all over this great city of ours. It was the motive behind why I had a nickel-plated 9mm Beretta in a police-issued holster (thanks to my dearest Alex) strapped to my side under my brown leather jacket.

CHAPTER 3:

Grades 9 and 10 (1993-1995)

The next two years of my life went by in a flash, like they never hap-pened. Sure, the bullying never stopped, but it was more of an afterthought than something happening in the present moment. The shoves against the lockers, constant taunting and teasing, head slaps and shin kicks, smashing of lunches into my face, and the ever-present *looking over my shoulder*, continued. But it was okay, really; you get used to it. It's kind of like how a prisoner gets used to their surroundings. At first, the continuous yelling and shouting and screaming and never ending ambient noise takes a toll on a them, but then it fades into the background…it becomes a part of everyday life; a non-issue. Survival is a daily task. Fighting against the demons in your head and the physical ones all around you develops into a subconscious task. It is—*normal.*

I had to take a Nietzschean approach to the whole thing. If it did not destroy me, then it had to make me stronger. I had to allow the core of all the pain and hurt and very public embarrassment create a tougher shell within my psyche and physical being.

A BULLIED REUNION

It did. I scored more goals on the pitch in the 9/10 season than anybody else in the history of the school. I averaged two goals per game and a couple of times I even put four into the back of the net—twice. I used my anger and studied furiously, receiving only top marks in *all* my classes—aces all the way. This not only impressed my father, who paid attention to what I was doing for once, but also my English 10 teacher. She submitted a short story I wrote to a major Canadian literary magazine in Vancouver and it was published in their spring issue. It was a 5000-word tale of a young boy who is tormented in high school and what he must do to cope. I received a letter from the editor of the publication inviting me to read at the Vancouver Writers Fest that was taking place at the Vancouver Art Gallery. So, it wasn't all bad… (Cue: "Every Rose Has Its Thorn"). Because of my exposure, I was able to submit one of my mom's poems to the same magazine—where she had already been rejected numerous times—and they were delighted to publish her work. It's who you know, right?

But it was during the latter part of Grade 10, right after I received the very nice letter from the editor, that the stupidest, most unthinkable thing happened. My dad thought it was a good idea to shave my head.

Let me explain: it was the first week in June and I had just gotten back from school. It was unusually hot and humid—twenty-five or twenty-six degrees outside—and the whole family was sweating. I'll admit, I was complaining the most. You see, our Tenth Avenue home was on a major roadway, so traffic was an absolute constant; it never let up. The heat from the cars, engines, and pavement was making me nauseous, so I decided to lie down on the couch in front of the television and just close my eyes for a bit. It was Friday afternoon after a long, hard week of school, early morning practices, and late nights studying, so I was tuckered out. I crashed—hard…

I was startled awake ninety minutes later to the sound of an electric trimmer and a cold sensation on the top of my head. My dad was giving me a buzz-cut. Right down to the scalp. A number ZERO. No plastic guard. Pure shears.

"What the hell, Dad?!" I bolted off the couch. The tip of the trimmer caught my eyebrow, so I started bleeding. "What're you doing?!"

His glossy eyes and stupid grin said he was drunk. He was completely bald, too, and he looked like a goof.

"Now we not so hot," he said, his deep accent more pronounced thanks to the booze.

I ran to the bathroom, knocking my five-year-old sister over on the way, and looked in the mirror. I had this strip of hair that was missing right down the centre and a couple of patches on the left side.

I heard him laughing in the other room. (He was lucky Mom wasn't home because she would have verbally kicked his ass all over the place.)

"Dad," I said, now back in the living room, "why did you do this to me?"

He just sat there on the couch with my sister on his lap. She was now crying because she got pushed down.

"It's cool, man. Be cool…like me." He tapped his head.

"How am I supposed to go to school like this?!" I screamed. I grabbed the trimmer and unplugged it. I had to finish the job but feared how the whole thing would turn out.

I went back into the bathroom, shook my head at the horror before me, and knew once I finished, I would be the laughing stock of the school for the remainder of the year. Even though it was only three weeks, in my world, it was a lifetime.

I clicked on the clippers. The thing vibrated angrily in my hand. I went from the front to back, front to back, cutting off every inch until there was just a little sandpaper-like grit left on top.

I finally looked like I felt: a prisoner.

On most kids, the skinhead look works. But on a head like mine, not so much. My head is disproportionate to the rest of my body. It is massively bulbous and round. I look like a lollipop.

"What the fuuuck?" Alex said as I walked onto the bus the next morning.

"I know," I said. "It's a stupid story."

"And one I gotta hear."

"You wouldn't believe me."

"Let me guess—your dad did it."

I nodded my head. "You know my life too well."

The moment I walked into the school, the snickers, jeers, and heckling started.

"Hey, look," Robert Cook said as he passed my locker right before first period, "it's Blossom and her bulging brain!"

Everyone around roared.

A BULLIED REUNION

"What?" he added, "You didn't find that funny?" He swept his hand over my head and slapped me hard. He walked away high-fiving a couple of students he did not know. They stuck their hands out anyway, afraid of the alternative if they didn't.

And so, for the rest of the day—and the balance of the week, actually—every time somebody looked my way, they had this goofy grin on their face. Even a few teachers couldn't help themselves and would cackle as I left the room. I was too embarrassed to tell them the truth. I just said that the "barber cut it too short" and left it at that.

I hated my dad now more than ever.

And I was glad—no, scratch that, I was ecstatic—when I came home that Friday afternoon and found him with his face in his hands, crying. Yes, crying. Fucking balling all over himself while my mother screamed constantly in Romanian about how "stupid" and "idiotic" he was. She used many of the same words he threw on me—payback's a bitch, ain't it?

"How are we going to pay the bills NOW?!" she screamed

Pay the bills…? What the fuck was going on?

"Everything okay?" I asked. "Why's Dad crying?"

"'Cause he's a stupid fucking drunk!" my mom replied.

When she spoke in English, I knew the shit had hit the fan. I've never seen my dad break down like that. He literally could not speak. He just sat there and cried.

"What happened?" I asked.

"He's a drunk." She threw her hands up in the hair in an *I-give-up* motion. "He's just a drunk…"

"Okay, I get it, but what's wrong? What—?"

My mom sat down at the kitchen table, back to my father, and told me that, in a nutshell, he was caught drinking at work. I still didn't know what he really did, but it was health research of some kind. He worked in a lab as a chemist. I guess the company was sold to some big investor in Alberta, and the son wanted to move the whole shebang to their home province. From what my mom said, they were going to hand out some hefty severance packages to those who could not, or would not, be making the move. Unfortunately, we would never see a dime because my dad's drinking problem had gone from bad to fucking insane. He tripped in front of his supervisor and the bottle of brandy he carried in the pocket of his lab coat shattered on the pristine white floor. They fired him on the spot and saved quite a bit of dough in the process. They had *cause*—no severance required. See ya.

Now my dad was out of work and a damn good reference. Getting fired from a prestigious private firm for boozing during business hours doesn't resonate on a resume.

"And now's he's crying," my mother said. "I should be the one crying." She left the room and slammed the bedroom door.

My dad finally stopped, stumbled to get up, and walked over to me. He whacked me as hard as he could across the face, open palm, with all the force his drunken body could muster.

* * *

Dad's drinking did not stop. He fell deeper and harder into his alcoholic hole. A month later, unable to make the rent, we moved into a two-bedroom apartment with my grandparents near Metrotown Centre. My sister and I slept on a pullout couch in the living room and my parents took one of the bedrooms.

Mom stayed home and took care of my sister, as usual, while my grandparents worked odd jobs cleaning buildings and delivering newspapers early in the morning. Grandpa even worked part-time at a pizza place—usually Friday and Saturday nights—that one of our Romanian friends owned. It was called *Roma Pizza* (how original) and it was right across the street from Metrotown, British Columbia's largest shopping complex.

Dad did nothing. He laid around all day and boozed away his time. After losing his job, he applied to a couple of competing firms, but nobody wanted anything to do with him after they made a call to his previous employer. He even applied at the hospital to work as a janitor. That fizzled when he showed up smelling like the inside of a whiskey barrel.

My mother never gave up on him. Even though my grandparents ignored him and never shared more than a couple of words to each other, Mom thought that somehow things would turn around, that he would find a good job, and that we would eventually move out of this cramped apartment.

Ah, yes, indeed. My mother, the naive optimist. The tortured poet who saw darkness in everything but believed she was the one who could shed a light on it all…

As the summer ended and my hair grew back just enough to make me look human, not like some anthropomorphic alien from another dimension, things were starting to look up.

"I did it!" Mom said as she walked through the doorway. "I did it! I did it!"

I was sitting on the couch with my sister, channel surfing.

"Whatcha do?" I asked.

She picked up my sister, who had just turned six a few weeks previous, and gave her a big kiss on the cheek, and then did the same to me (without the picking up part).

"I got the job!" She was standing in front of the TV, both hands in the air, like a giddy high school cheerleader.

"What job?" I asked, completely confused.

She looked like she got a new haircut. It was black, shiny, and short. She wore a navy-blue suit with a white silk dress shirt underneath. She looked like a lawyer. I had never seen her so polished, sober, and fresh.

She let out a deep breath and said, "At the bank. They hired me at the bank!"

My grandparents walked in the door. Grandpa carried the same energy Mom had. He was the same height—a little over six feet and completely bald on top. Whatever hair he had on the sides he shaved clean with a razor. Grandma was wearing a long, flower-patterned dress that made her look emaciated, like she was just released from a concentration camp. Her hair was as white as the clouds and she had the bluest ocean eyes you ever saw on an eastern European.

"I won!" Grandpa said in Romanian.

"We won!" said Grandma, also in Romanian.

They were both smiling, all teeth, from ear to hear. Grandpa hugged Mom and Grandma wrapped her arms around our heads and squeezed.

My mom backed away, asked Grandpa, "What did you win?"

He handed her a one-dollar *Scratch & Win* ticket he bought along with the groceries at the corner store on his way home. She looked carefully at the ticket. I got up to look, too. It was a winner! It had three sections scratched off that had various monetary values in each: $25 / $1000 / $500. The common thread, of course, was that it had $10,000 matching in each one!

The bonus game said NOT A WINNER. But at this point, who cared?

My mom burst out crying. She hugged Grandpa and then told him the good news (in Romanian) about her new job. She would start Tuesday, the day after Labour Day.

The first day back to school.

CHAPTER 4:

Twenty Year High School Reunion (2017)

They were the only three at the cash bar. Most everyone else was either dancing or already had their drinks in hand. But Jeremy Freemont, Robert Cook, and Michael Underwood were just getting it started. They hammered it up with the attractive brunette bartender whose enormous tits they couldn't stop staring at. She smiled and pushed her chest out. She wore black slacks and a tight, white dress shirt that had the top four buttons undone; all cleavage and skin.

"So, what can I get for you gentlemen?" she finally asked.

"Well—" Jeremy looked closely at her nametag pinned above her left breast, as if he were blind, "Jessica, I'll have a rum and Coke, no ice, no lime." He slammed a ten on the portable bar top.

"I'll have the same," Robert interjected, pushing in toward the bar, getting as close as possible, "but lotsa ice, in a big glass."

"And for you," she called out to Michael.

"Heineken," Underwood said, paying no attention to the flirting. He was more interested in the crowd. Who was here? Who wasn't?

Jeremy and Rob grabbed their drinks and Rob handed Michael his beer. "Here," he said, "You get the next one."

Michael nodded in agreement, downed almost half, and kept scanning the room. "I'm gonna fuck her," he said, tipping his head back toward the bartender.

"I'm sure you will," Rob replied.

They clinked their drinks together.

"To twenty more," Jeremy said.

"Fucking rights," Michael agreed.

They turned and stood in a perfect row, lined up as if they were about to executed.

CHAPTER 5:

Grade 11 (1995-1996)

"We're gonna learn some pretty cool shit in this class," Alex said. She sat next to me in the second row. Usually, she's a back row kind of gal, but I guess Western Civilization 11 ignited a learning flame in her.

"It's like a beefed-up Social Studies class," I replied.

Everyone sat at their desk on Day One, Block A as the first bell rang. It would only be a half-day, as in past years. The same old process with the same old students and the same old teachers—

"Good morning, everyone."

What? It couldn't be! It was her!

"Can you help me pass out these textbooks?" Miss Diamond asked a couple of students in the front two rows.

Alex turned her head to the left, looking at me, waiting to see my reaction. She whispered, "Well, there you go, lover boy…"

Miss Lena Diamond looked right at me and smiled. She recognized who I was right away. She waved with a quick flutter of fingers.

I couldn't breathe. My throat felt like I had swallowed an eggplant. I had seen her quite a few times at the pool over the years, but we only said "Hello" and "See ya later" in passing. We never carried on a conversation. I was too fucking shy.

But I hadn't forgotten about her. *Never.*

"I hope everyone had a great summer," Miss Diamond said. She leaned back against her big wooden desk, her ankles crossed.

She wore a red summer tank dress cut just above the knee with a white floral pattern and a matching head scarf that made her look like she was from the '60s. I couldn't believe how much she resembled the chick who jumped out of a cake in that Steven Seagal movie where Tommy Lee Jones took an entire aircraft carrier hostage. She could have been her twin. Her breasts bulged now more than ever, and the skin on her arms was flawlessly tanned. Her beauty carried the scent of perfection.

I wanted to consume her in every which way possible. My sixteen-year-old mind was sprinting with steamy sex scenes. I was looking right at her—her lips were moving but I couldn't hear a word she was saying.

"Cristiano?" she said. "Hello?" She waved her hand at me.

Shit.

"Sorry," I said, "I spaced-out for a sec."

"Bored already?" A pause. "Am I not exciting enough for you?" She smirked, raised her eyebrows, then pouted her lips, crossed her arms and pushed her breasts up.

Most students were flipping through textbooks as soon as it hit their desks, not paying attention to her flirtatiousness. I felt a little uncomfortable. Luckily, Rob, Jeremy, nor Michael were in this class, or they would have ripped me for it.

Miss Diamond walked toward the blackboard and began listing the different topics and chapters we were going to cover—from the Roman Empire to the Renaissance to the Industrial Revolution.

"Gee, that was subtle," Alex said.

"I know, right?" I replied. I was flattered but fearful; unsure and unnerved.

Miss Diamond began to describe the course: what percentage assignments were worth, in class quizzes and essays, and, finally, the final exam, which would account for forty percent of our grade. Every head in the room was bobbing up and down, writing and concentrating and copying the contents of the chalkboard into their notebooks. The bell rang as she turned and

A BULLIED REUNION

said, "My door's always open. So, if you need to see me—" she looked my way, "just *come.*"

* * *

Wow. It was already noon.

First day of Grade 11: COMPLETE. Alex was already at our shared locker. (We managed, through no influence of mine, to be locker partners since Grade 8.) It was directly across the hall from Miss Diamond's classroom.

"Hey, cowboy," Alex said.

"Cowboy?" I replied. "Really?"

Alex, in her best Texas twang, said, "That little missy over there—" she nodded toward Miss Diamond, who was sitting at her desk, scribbling, "wants a ride on your saddle."

"You're really fucked up, you know that?" I said.

I looked back into the classroom. Miss Diamond quickly took out a pre-scription pill bottle from her purse, dumped two into her palm, and washed them down with what looked to be stale coffee from a mug that said **"I GOT LEI'D IN MAUI."**

"Quit staring," Alex said, "you'll grow hair on your palms."

"Very funny," I said. I put my books at the top end of the locker, grabbed my backpack, and shut the door. "You ready?"

She gave me the hang-loose sign and said, "Let's blitz."

This year the school was trying to be creative, so they changed the sched-ule a bit. Mondays, Tuesdays, and Thursdays would be normal: Block **A** then **B** then **C** then **D**; but Wednesdays and Fridays would switch to **B** then **D** then **C** then **A**. This meant that I would either *start* the day with the lovely Miss Diamond or *end* it. Both scenarios were extremely desirable and welcomed.

None of this would start until the second week of school so, for now, it was the standard **A** / **B** / **C** / **D** order. On the second day of school, a brightly happy and sunny Wednesday morning, I decided to surprise Miss Diamond with a little something.

Since we moved into our apartment, Mom had this ritual where she would take me to school every morning and then grab a coffee from Starbucks on her way home. She got ready and went to work at the TD Bank from ten till six. This morning, though, I asked if she could switch things up a bit and go to Starbucks first.

"How come?" she asked.

"I dunno, I just feel like a coffee, something sweet," I replied.

"Since when do you drink coffee?" She made a left into the Starbucks parking lot about two blocks south from our apartment.

YES!

"I just thought I'd try something new," I said, mentally fist-pumping.

My mom, an avid java drinker and somewhat of a coffee connoisseur, did not protest. If her son wanted to take a glimpse into her world, who was she to stop me?

It was my first time inside a Starbucks. The menu was massive. They had more choices than most fast food joints—and this was only coffee! Jeez. The gal at the register knew all the regulars and promptly greeted my mother. "Hello, good morning, Angelica," she said. "Venti coffee, room for cream?"

"Yes, thank you," she said and smiled.

"And who is this?" the barista asked.

"My son, *The Virgin*," my mother replied with a little sass in her voice.

"Mom!" I said, but then realized she meant it as *untouched* in the coffee world, not the sexual one. Sadly, both were correct.

The barista's nametag told the world her name was Melinda. She was around twenty-one or twenty-two, with short hair cropped in the back, and long, knife-cut bangs in the front, parted to the left and just barely touching her cheekbone. She had a massive smile and a clean, fresh face that looked like it never saw a speck of dirt or acne.

"Well, I'm honoured to pop your cherry this morning," she said, winking playfully.

I smiled along with her. "I'd like something sweet," I said, "like in that picture."

"Tall Caramel Macchiato—coming right up!" She took a sharpie and began to write something on the cup. "What was your name?"

"Cris is fine," I said, not realizing she probably didn't know my full name anyway.

"He sure is," she said, and winked *again*.

My mom looked at me and raised her eyebrows a couple of times. "Oh-la-la," she whispered.

It was nice to see her sober and happy. She was making good money and taking care of herself.

She paid for our drinks and we lined up behind the rest of the morning slugs waiting for their fix. And after a couple of minutes our order was up. "Venti coffee!" another barista shouted out. "And a Tall Caramel Macchiato!"

We grabbed our drinks, my mom waved to Melinda—who blew me a kiss—and we left.

"Since when do you drink coffee?" Alex asked.

"It's not for me," I replied.

She looked bright-eyed and bushy-tailed this morning. Her hair was slicked back into a fiery ponytail. She wore painted-on blue jeans, a pair of black Doc Martens with a white top that said **SEX PISTOLS** underneath a black- and red-checkered flannel shirt that looked like it once belonged to a forestry worker.

"Let me guess: it's for Miss Horny Pants over there—" she nodded toward the classroom.

"I'm just being friendly, okay?" I said.

"Dude, you know that's creepy, right?" she said.

"What's creepy? She's super nice. And so am I."

Alex gave me this long, belaboured look of frustration. "Funny enough, I was watchin' the news last night—yeah, I know, the news, I was bored, okay?—and there was this teacher chick down in Texas who got convicted of having sex with one of her students, and so she ended up doing some time, and this kid who she's fucking jumps out of his apartment window and kills himself 'cause he can't be with her...now that's fucked up."

I stared in utter confusion. "What does that even mean?" I asked, not really wanting a response. "You know what? I gotta go..." I carried my textbook and binder under my left arm and my morning treat for Ms. Diamond in my right hand, upright and ready to present it to her as I turned away from Alex.

I instantly made eye contact with Miss Diamond. She saw me coming toward her classroom, door wide open. I had on my best pair of blue jeans, white Adidas indoor soccer shoes, and a white Umbro tee; I was totally stylin'. Sporty and cool. Short and sweet.

"This is so fucked up." I heard Alex say behind me. "Don't go jumping out any windows…" She faded into the background.

I was two steps from the classroom door when I felt someone kick my right heel into my left ankle.

I tripped. I fell. The drink crushed and exploded underneath me when it hit the ground; coffee and caramel and foam soaked my chest.

"Oh, my, god!" Miss Diamond said, leaping off her chair and toward me.

I heard snickering in the background as I got up. The front of my shirt looked like vomit.

"Look at you," Miss Diamond said, next to me now. "Are you okay?"

"I'm fine," I said. Then something inside me *snapped*. I didn't care anymore. I didn't care about my shirt, my pants, my books, my gift to Miss Diamond, my life, my anything. Everything turned dark red in front of me. It suddenly felt hot. All I could hear was this high-pitched ringing sound. Like someone was blowing a dog whistle and I was the only one who could hear it.

I saw Underwood furiously walking away, about to make a right into another classroom. I sprinted as hard as I could and tackled him from behind just before he made the turn. He was probably close to six feet and weighed sixty to seventy pounds more than I did, but the insane rage that encompassed me was demonic. I could have stopped a moving train if I had to.

Once I had him on the ground, I pounded the back of his head as hard as I could, hoping to knock the motherfucker out. But he easily turned his body and rolled around underneath me, thrusted his hips upward and bounced me over and onto my back. (I completely forgot that besides football, he had been on the wrestling team for the past three years.) Once he had me flat and was on top, he struck me once in the face, squarely on the nose, and then somehow crawled up and around my body and started choking me from behind.

It all happened so fast. All I remember was Miss Diamond standing over us as I started to fade to black. She was screaming for Michael to let me go. But Underwood had his headlock in deep and was not going to let go until I went off into la-la land…

A BULLIED REUNION

Which I did, in about three seconds flat.

And then I pissed my pants.

An hour later we were both in the principal's office. I had changed into my soccer uniform.

Underwood smirked at me as we waited for Mr. Price to show up. (He was speaking with Miss Diamond in another office.)

"I'm gonna make you eat my shit," Underwood said to me.

I had a tissue balled up underneath my nose trying to stop the continual flow of blood. I said, "Why?" My eyes were teary. "Why won't you just leave me alone? Why do you and your friends hate me so much?"

"Gentlemen," Mr. Price said as he walked into his office, "can someone please tell me what happened?" He closed the door behind him and sat at his desk.

I was tired of talking. Tired of trying to make the staff understand what was going on without actually spilling the beans about the situation completely, knowing that it would only aggravate the situation. So, I just stood there, silent.

Michael spoke up, "We were just messin' around, Mr. Price."

"*Messin' around*?" Mr. Price repeated.

"Yeah, it's not serious or nothin'. We was just, you know, playin'."

"Miss Diamond seems to think otherwise," Mr. Price said. "She says you tripped Cristiano and then you"—he nodded to me—"tackled him. After which you"—now nodding back to Michael—"then choked him unconscious. That's not *messin' around* in my books."

I did not know what to do or say. Do I burn Underwood and unleash hell? Or do I sit back and just let this take its natural course?

"It's my fault, Mr. Price," I said. I thought of an escape route that would put me in the bad books but might get Underwood off my back. I looked to my left, directly at Michael, and said, "I called him a *nigger* this morning… that's why he tripped me. I started the whole thing." (I didn't have a racist bone in my body. And it was the first time I ever said that word out loud. It hurt, and I thought I made the wrong move. But I knew it was horrible enough to take the spotlight off Michael and shine it on me.)

Underwood gave me a look that said *what the fuck are you doing?* before he quickly realized what my plan was.

Mr. Price, being not only black, but also involved in every single anti-racism campaign and rally and cause in existence, would instantly take the heat off Michael for what he did and put the fire back on my lap. "You what?" he said.

"I'm sorry," I said to Underwood. "I shouldn't have called you that. I was just mad about you hitting on Alex." I made this up as I went along...

Underwood and Price looked at each other, then at me. Underwood said, "It's cool. It's all right...you didn't mean it. Whatever."

"Mean it or not, this type of language is unacceptable." Mr. Price was skeptical. He raised his right eyebrow and leaned over onto his desk like he was about to call me out. Instead, he said "I want you to finish out the day and then come see me. Now get out of here."

"I'm sorry," I said as I got up.

I left the office and headed back to my locker.

"I don't know what the hell is going on," Mr. Price said to Michael Underwood, "but this smells like bullshit. And I don't like being played the fool. There's no way that kid called you a nigger. So, whatever you're doing to him, or whatever the truth is, I want it to stop, right here and right now."

Michael smirked arrogantly and said, "You want me to stop telling the truth?"

"I beg your pardon?"

"You said, *whatever the truth is*, you want it to stop, *right here and right now.*"

"You have no idea how thin the ice is."

Underwood said, "Can I go now?"

"I know you've been riding that kid pretty hard. But it's over. You're done. You don't talk to him, you don't acknowledge him. He doesn't exist. Got it?"

"Can I go now?" he asked again, looking up at the ceiling.

Mr. Price stood up, placed both palms on his desk, and leaned forward. "You touch that kid again and I'll put my foot so far up your ass you'll have a leather tongue." Underwood sat completely still. "Now get the fuck out of my office."

Underwood left.

A BULLIED REUNION

Principal Price pressed his intercom and said, "Celia, page Jeremy Freemont and Robert Cook. Have them come to my office immediately."

* * *

I got to my locker and saw that Miss Diamond's Western Civ. 11 door was closed. I could hear her teaching on the other side. I did not want to head back in wearing a soccer uniform. Looking like a total dweeb. After pissing myself. Jesus...fuck...

But I knew I couldn't just stand here all day, either. So, I opened my locker, grabbed my bag and headed out the back door...fuck it, I was out of here...

* * *

"So, you just left?" Alex asked. She called me the moment she got home.

"I couldn't go back to class..." I was sitting on the couch in our apartment. Nobody was home yet. It was stone quiet. "I fucking pissed myself, Alex."

"I heard that right before you die you piss *and* shit yourself. You lose all bowel functions."

"And that's supposed to make me feel better?"

"Well...how about this: I don't know if you heard or not, but Jeremy *and* Robert were both paged to the office, right after you left."

"Are you serious?"

"Totally."

"Shit..."

"Yeah, shit. Maybe they'll finally stop."

"Don't bet on it." I let out a deep breath. "I was supposed to meet with Mr. Price after school..."

"And you ditched? Not so good..."

"No, not so good at all. But, whatever."

"You know, Cris, you can't just *whatever* the next two years of your life. This is real. You've gotta deal with this and end it. It's getting stupid."

83

I looked out the balcony window: a blue jay landed on the railing and was bobbing its head up and down. It looked stressed about something. Nervous, even. I said, "I'm gonna get through high school. I'm gonna go to university. And then I'll never have to see those fucking assholes again. Because they'll never amount to anything. They'll be building *my* dream house—Underwood'll be putting up *my* drywall. Those fuckers'll be taking out *my* garbage—like the fucking trash they are."

"They'll be pumping *our* gas," Alex added. "They'll be mopping *our* floors and cleaning *our* gutters."

We both laughed at our intensity.

"Yeah—fuck 'em," I said.

∗   ∗   ∗

Thursday morning: day three of Grade 11. Enough had happened already to send most kids off the deep end. I mean, how do you recover socially from having pissed yourself in front of a bunch of students *after* being choked unconscious? Well…it was a good thing that socially I didn't give a fuck. I had no "social life" except for the soccer team—who only seemed to acknowledge my existence while on the playing field, during games. Alex, as usual, was the only person I ever spoke to during school hours. And now, to add insult to my injury, I had to face Principal Price's wrath for not showing up to our meeting. I don't think he liked being stood up.

"Cristiano—telephone!" my mom yelled from the kitchen. Everybody was already awake, so it didn't matter. "It's your principal!"

Huh? Mr. Price? Shit. He must be pissed off if he's calling me at home. Fuck. I ran to the kitchen and Mom handed me the phone.

"Hello?" I said with trepidation.

"What do you say I pick you up today?" Mr. Price asked.

"Pick me up?" I answered.

"For school. I'll buy you breakfast. We'll do a drive-thru."

I looked at the clock on the stove. It said 7:03 a.m.

"Yeah, sure, that'd be great," I said.

"Good. I'll see you in thirty minutes."

A BULLIED REUNION

The buzzer for the door downstairs went off promptly at 7:33 a.m.

"I'll be right down," I said into the wall-mounted intercom system. "Bye, Mom—love ya," I said as I ran out the door. (I rarely ever saw my dad before school. He had a job delivering newspapers with my grandpa. It was a sick, early morning route that they had to get up for at 3:30.)

Mr. Price was sitting in his car in our apartment building's little round-about tapping the steering-wheel with both hands and shaking his head side-to-side. The bass thumped.

I opened the passenger door and was instantly hit with TLC's "Waterfalls."

"Good morning, young fella," Mr. Price said.

"Morning, Mr. Price," I replied.

He turned down the volume just as T-Boz was admonishing us to stick to the rivers that we are used to. "What do you feel like? Mickey D's or A&W?"

"Mickey's sounds good," I said.

"Then Mickey's it is," he said.

We ordered breakfast burritos, hash browns, and coffee with room for cream. I thought I would save my coffee and give it to Miss Diamond. A lesser replacement from yesterday's high-value Caramel Macchiato, but would still be welcomed.

We sat in his car in the staff parking lot behind the school, dipping our burritos in the small plastic container of picante sauce.

With his mouth full, Mr. Price asked, "How come you never came to us?"

"About what?" I replied.

"About what? Come on. About all this going on with you and Underwood. I know he's been on your ass for a while."

Yeah, the past three goddamn years! "I dunno—I just thought it was *my* business. Nobody else's," I said.

"Well, it's mine, now, too. And I'm sorry if we ignored it. We—I—have a lot to deal with. There are twelve hundred students that walk through those doors every single day." He wiped sauce off his lower lip with a napkin. "And you're not the only one who's being bullied. It's tough for us to really do anything except warn or suspend a student if it's serious. Which, in your case, it wasn't too bad…"

Wasn't too bad?! If he only knew the half of it. "You don't have to make any excuses, Mr. Price. I never told anyone anything. It's just the way things are."

85

"I'm not making any excuses. I'm telling you that's the way it is. And yesterday it got beyond just locker shoves and teasing."

Oh, it's been beyond that for quite a while, you ignorant fuck.

"So," he said, looking like he was about to finish his verbal dissertation, "I promise that I'll keep a closer eye on things, okay?"

"I appreciate that," I said.

"You're a great kid," he said. "And I don't want to see this whole high school thing ruin you. So, let it toughen you up, all right? Use it as a motivator to ensure you do great things in life. Because the last time I checked, you're the smartest one in that building. Your marks are top tier. And you're a damn good athlete."

"Thanks. That means a lot," I said. I couldn't have cared less about Mr. Price's little motivational minute. All I could think of was how cold Miss Diamond's coffee was getting.

"Well…I'm glad we had this talk," he said while scrunching up his burrito wrappers and gulping down another swallow of his big brew. "Now, you come see me right away if anything else happens, okay?"

"You bet," I replied.

"Good." He patted me on the chest with his open palm, opened his door, and walked toward the back entrance of the school.

I sat in his car for another minute. And then, as I opened the car door, I saw Jeremy Freemont huddled in the smoke pit, near the garbage bins; he took a big drag off his cigarette and said, "Whatcha doin', Blossom? Givin' the old man a blow job?"

* * *

"It's a little cold," I said to Miss Diamond, minutes before the bell was about to ring, "but it's good."

She wore a light brown sweater with a huge opening around her neck, and sometimes it would slide off her left shoulder, exposing gloriously smooth and tan skin underneath a black bra strap. I inhaled the fragrant lavender or lilac (or whatever) she rubbed all over herself.

"Well, thank you," she said, caressing my arm. "That's so sweet. I actually didn't get a chance to make one at home. And I wouldn't call what we have in the staff room *coffee*. It's more like tar and water." She smiled. Her teeth were like brilliantly white priceless pearls. Her breasts jutted out and rounded themselves perfectly through her top.

I wanted to touch her. I wanted to smell her. I wanted to explore every inch and crevasse. I took my seat and waited for the rest of the class to arrive. Miss Diamond took a couple of big sips, placed her coffee on the edge of her desk, and began writing on the board. As students started walking through the doors, I heard an announcement over the PA system.

"Good morning, everyone," Mr. Price began. "Just a quick announcement: we're going to have an unscheduled assembly today right after first break. All students and teachers are required to attend. Thank you."

Miss Diamond turned around and looked at the class. Her jeans were once again painted on. Her swimmer's thighs—muscular and tight—looked as if they were ready to burst through. She wore these sandals that looked gladiatorial, almost biblical in their style. They made her feet look heavenly.

Written on the board, in big bold letters was **Sex & Sand: The Study of Ancient Egypt**.

She clasped her hands together and asked, "Everyone ready to dive in?"

I looked right at her and knew I was already in the deep end.

*　*　*

Almost 1300 of us crammed into the gym—sitting on the floor, on the bleachers, standing around the outer walls—waiting for the assembly to begin.

Miss Lang was up on stage with thirty other students. She spoke into the microphone attached to the wooden, pulpit-like podium: "We are going to sing in French and you follow along in English—okay?"

Mrs. Camden played the small electric KORG up on stage as we belted out "O Canada." You couldn't really hear the French version, even with Ms. Lang crooning on the microphone. L'anglais dominated.

We sat down as Mr. Price took to the podium.

He cleared his throat and began. "Thank you everyone for being here." (Did we really have a choice?) "This year, I'd like to start by doing something a little different. I know that usually we have a year-end assembly where we honour outstanding students and their achievements, but this year I'd like to begin with an inspirational bang, so to speak, and look at two new categories, or awards, if you will."

Students looked around at one another, not sure what he was talking about.

"At the end of last year, we gave out certificates of achievement for students who made the honour roll, for those that had an outstanding athletic year in each and every division or sport, and for students who went above and beyond in their volunteer work, or who helped teachers and other students with everyday school work or assignments.

"We will still have our assembly at the end of every year, but in addition, at the start of the semester, we are going to have an assembly, like this one, that will welcome new students to the school, wish those that are in their final year a successful and pleasant one, and present any new school policy changes, upcoming events, or introduce any new teachers that have recently come on board with us here at BCSS. So, without further ado, I'd like to officially welcome all the new grade eights to our wonderful school. Eights, would you all please stand."

As students shuffled and stood, the natural progression of applause resounded throughout the room.

"Please remain standing," Mr. Price continued. "Students, teachers, and faculty members, I want you to look very carefully at each individual. At each person…at each student." It was completely silent as he paused. "Because this is the future. This is where it all begins. This is where we must start setting a precedent. Number one, first and foremost, we have, as of today, something we should have addressed publicly a long time ago…a ZERO tolerance for bullying."

The couple hundred eights blinked like lost deer in the woods.

"We, as a school, DO NOT accept hateful words, racial slurs, or swearing on school premises. Physical contact between students—or teachers—in a hurtful manner, like shoving, pushing, tripping, or touching of any kind, is not allowed. Essentially, all forms of verbal or physical intimidation are completely improper, not only on school property, but out in the real world,

A BULLIED REUNION

as well. It's not the way a student of ours should represent themselves within the community."

He cleared his throat again and took a sip of water. "Furthermore, if any student is caught in violation of any of the above, they will be given one warning. A letter will be sent to their parents or guardians clearly outlining the infraction. A second warning will not come. Two infractions are grounds for immediate expulsion. And this is not up for debate. We are taking the next step in our evolution as a school"—he raised his voice an octave—"Burnaby Central Senior Secondary will become a BULLY-FREE ZONE this year and for years and years to come!"

Everybody jumped to their feet and applauded for the better part of a minute. Mr. Price raised both hands in the air—like a healing evangelist conducting a mass crusade—and said, "And this is all fine and dandy. And I'm glad—ecstatic, actually—over the enthusiasm that has prevailed here this morning, but this applause *must* translate into action if we are to see a significant change in our school."

All of us applauded again and even a few whistles broke out among the crowd, with shouts of "Yes, yes!"

For once, I saw that I was not alone. There were other students around me crying and wiping tears from their eyes. (I had been so cocooned within my own little world that I never really noticed the torture and torment others must have endured as well…)

Mr. Price smiled. He believed his words resonated within our hearts and that maybe a change would occur. He looked around the room at all the faces and spotted mine.

"One student," he said, "that has excelled amid what I am talking about is standing right here among you."

Oh, no. What the hell is he doing?!

"He is the one I'd like to honour this morning. And this is something I will do at the beginning of each and every school year. But it's not so much about singling out any one individual as it is about showing the rest of the student body what is truly possible. So, what I'd like to do is present Cristiano Leuca with an Outstanding Achievement award for his accomplishments during his grade ten year. Cristiano, would you please come to the stage."

Massive, resounding applause carried me to the front of the gym and up the wooden steps to the main stage.

I stood next to Mr. Price, he shook my hand, and hugged me. (He hugged me!)

"This young man," he began, "finished his grade ten year with not only the highest marks in his grade, but the highest marks in the entire school."

I looked at all the faces as applause rang through and was surprised to see how many students were smiling up at me. Alex winked and gave me a thumbs up.

"His lowest grade" (Mr. Price paused for effect) "—and we won't say in which class"—a little laughter from the crowd—"was 98.9%. The rest were 100%."

(Applause)

"During this time," Mr. Price went on, "he also broke the school record for most goals scored in one season by a single player on our soccer team—with a total of thirty-two goals last year!"

As another round of applause clapped on, he handed me two certificates with big gold stickers on the bottom that noted my success as a well-rounded student.

"And from now on," Mr. Price said, "we will begin the year just like this. With an award for an outstanding student and one for the outstanding athlete from the previous school year. This year it just so happens that those two awards go to one student. And it is his alone to cherish."

Miss Diamond shouted from the side wall, "Speech! Speech!"

Encouraging shouts and whistles rang out. Mr. Price patted me on the shoulder and pushed me toward the podium. It looked like I had no choice in the matter. I was going to have to say something.

I gripped the side of the podium and felt as though I was going to topple over. "There's not really much I can say," I began nervously, "except that I'm really"—I cleared my throat—"honoured to be recognized this morning. I know a lot of you don't really *know* me too well, but I hope this changes things. That we really can become a school that watches each other's backs. And that we don't allow those that are bigger or stronger to bully their way into our lives and ruin whatever precious memories we're trying to create here. Because I believe these years we have together should be some of the best of our entire lives."

A BULLIED REUNION

I paused for a moment to gauge the crowd. They were listening intently. (For my first public speech, I was doing all right…it looked like I had their complete attention and they were eating out of the palm of my hand.)

"So, let's try to not only be nice to one another, but to protect each other, too. The only way we can do that is by opening our eyes and being aware of what's happening around us all the time. If you see someone being treating in a negative way, report to a teacher. If you see another student bullying or intimidating or making fun of another student, or you see someone doing something that you wouldn't want done to you, report it right away. Because bullying is gross—and that's not who we are as a school." I raised my voice and shouted: "We are bigger and better than that!"

The roar and applause matched that of Mr. Price's earlier. He gave me another big squeeze and took to the podium.

"As you can see," he said, "we are all of the same mind. Your applause and enthusiasm prove this is an issue we *will* conquer. And that the answers are right here, in this room. It's our attitude that determines our direction. Some of you are almost done and others are just beginning. But wherever you are in your journey, let's make it a great one!"

* * *

After the assembly, Mr. Price wanted us all to go back to our **B** blocks and discuss ways ("brainstorm" was the word he used) to ensure our success with respect to student togetherness and school spirit. I had Math 11 with Mr. Woo, so the timing was perfect…

Students greeted me at lunchtime as I walked down the hall with "Awesome job, man!" and "Your speech was really cool." Even a grade twelve student said, "I gotchyourback, bro."

Overwhelmed and surprised, I entered the cafeteria, where students from all grades asked me to sit with them. Complete strangers just hours ago, now wanted to be my best buddies…

I sat with Alex, who was next to a couple of my teammates (who actually spoke with me now outside of the normal confines of the soccer pitch). I was sure that by the final bell my back would be black and blue from all the pats and slaps I received.

CHRIS PONICI

*   *   *

The next couple of months went by as if I was caught in a perfect dream. The Amigos didn't say one word to me. It was like I didn't even exist, which was perfectly fine with me. I was dubbed "Mini Maradona" by the soccer team. This was also perfectly fine with me. Anything other than "Blossom."

"What are you going as for the Halloween Dance?" Alex asked. We were at our locker, grabbing textbooks for our Block C class; English for me and Foods for Alex. It was Friday and the dance was Halloween night, this coming Tuesday.

"I don't know yet," I said. "But I was thinking about going as a shower. Like in *The Karate Kid*."

"Really? That's cheesy."

"I think it's original," I countered.

"How could it be original if someone's already done it?"

"It's original because nobody'll be wearing it. I mean, how many vampires and sexy kittens and zombies do you think we'll see?"

"Sexy kitten...not a bad idea.... Everyone loves a little pussy—"

"Hey, you two," Ms. Diamond said as she stepped out of her classroom and walked toward us. "You coming to the Halloween dance?"

Alex and I both nodded. "Yeah, it should be fun. You?" Alex said.

"Absolutely," she said. "I love Halloween. It's the only time you get to be whoever you want for a whole night. And you can go crazy and nobody cares." She had on this mischievous smirk, like she was the high schooler and we were the teachers.

The bell rang.

"I'll see you both last period," she said, waving us off.

"I wonder what she'll go as..." I said to Alex as we walked down the hallway.

"That'd be one sexy kitten..."

*   *   *

A BULLIED REUNION

"Thanks again for the ride, Mrs. Leuca," Alex said as my mother pulled up in front of the school.

"Anytime, sweetie pie. You just have fun, okay?" my mother replied.

"Thanks, Mom," I said just before I closed the rear door.

"Be careful coming home on the bus—it could be stupid tonight." She pulled away blowing us kisses, honking, and waving. She's the best.

"You know what?" Alex said, looking me up and down. "You actually look pretty cool. And kinda cute. I think you might get some action tonight…"

I shook my head. She was always trying to set me up. She couldn't believe I was still a virgin and hadn't even kissed a girl yet.

I was wearing my *Star Trek: The Next Generation* Commander William Riker uniform I bought at a convention in August. It was red, just like on the TV show. I thought it would be less cumbersome and easier to navigate than the shower Ralph Macchio wore.

We walked up the stairs to the main entrance where a bunch of ghouls and ghosts were making their way inside. The hallway was completely dark except for a few strobe lights placed on the floor that flickered through thick smoke that hovered just below our feet.

Coolio's "Gangsta's Paradise" slammed us in the chest as Alex and I opened the main gym doors. There were two smoke machines on stage along with red and blue and green lights that pulsated and waved around to each beat.

"That's fuckin' cool," Alex said.

The DJ (a grade twelve student) then faded into Montell Jordan's "This Is How We Do It" and the packed gymnasium—twelves and elevens only—started jumping up and down. Zombies, vampires, and pumpkins threw their hands up as if this was the greatest night of their lives.

When Alex found out that her major crush was going as the Big Bad Wolf, she decided to dress up as Little Red Riding Hood. She wore black shoes, white stockings, and a short blue dress with a red-hooded coat.

"There he is—" Alex said, pointing to a student with a massive head, huge nose, and full fur. He looked like a university mascot; more silly than scary. "I'll see you in a bit."

"Yeah, okay," I said, knowing I probably wouldn't see her again until it was time to leave. Guys were the focus of her life lately—

"Well, look at you!"

I turned around and who should I see but—

"Hey, Miss Diamond," I said. I was blown away. She was wearing her red lifeguard swimsuit, with skin-colored coloured tights that were cut off at the ankle so she could slip into her matching red flip-flops. A big, blond, over-the-top wig—poofed up higher than Dolly Parton's coif—sat atop her head. In her right hand she held one of those red plastic flotation devices.

"I'm a dumb lifeguard. Like those *Baywatch* babes," she said. She had just arrived. She was looking around and taking it all in. "This is pretty wild."

There were fake spider webs hanging everywhere, and dozens of glow in the dark bats taped to the walls.

"Your costume looks great," I said, shouting a bit over the music, "just like on the TV show." I was incredibly shy now and very uncomfortable.

"Yeah, you too!" she replied. "Which one are you? The Captain?"

I shook my head. "I'm Commander Riker." I had Mom use this black dye on my hair that would wash out in the morning and she also glued a fake beard onto my face.

"Sorry," she said, in close to my ear now, "I don't really watch that show."

I felt awkward seeing her again in her bathing suit. I had not been to the aquatic centre in over a year.

She lifted her flotation device onto her shoulder like a lumberjack would with his axe, and said, "I'll see you a bit later, okay?" A delightful fragrance emanated from her perfectly hairless armpit when she leaned in to talk to me.

I wanted to kiss her there. Right in the sweetness of her pit. I was slowly getting hard. Not a good idea with the costume I was wearing: it was just as skintight as her bathing suit.

"Yeah, for sure," I said, quickly walking away. I didn't turn around until I reached the far wall opposite the stage, where all the drinks and finger-foods were laid out.

I danced to some fast songs—"Cotton Eye Joe" by Rednex; "Run Away" by The Real McCoy; and Shaggy's "Boombastic"—with Alex and her friends and a few guys on my soccer team. We were in a big circle and hopped and jumped around to whatever beat was bumping through the massive speakers.

After about an hour and a half of laughter and crazy dance moves, the DJ said: "We're saving the best for last...students, go grab your favourite teacher for the final slow dance."

I don't know if it was all the sugary pop I drank or the euphoria from the music and cardiovascular output from the dancing and jumping, but I felt confident and sure of myself. I had some friends now. And we laughed. And we had a good time. And life was pretty damn good. So, I did it. I saw that absolutely nobody had the guts to go over to Ms. Diamond—who was speaking to another teacher and holding a red Dixie cup—and ask her to dance.

I strode confidently in her direction and she saw me heading her way! As I was about ten feet away, this kid in a football uniform, helmet, and pads, said a few words to her and grabbed her by the hand. She gave me the *I'm so sorry* look and kept on with this other kid. Vanessa Williams' iconic "Save the Best for Last" played as Miss Diamond and this other unknown entity stood between us.

All I could do was lean up against the wall and watch. I was sweating badly, and my beard was coming loose. I ripped it off and threw it into the trashcan. That's when I saw him. It was Jeremy Freemont. He had his greasy hands on Miss Diamond's waist and she had hers draped over his shoulder pads. He must have stunk like crazy in that football gear. He looked right at me and mouthed the words: *Fuck you, Blossom.*

The lights came up at the end of the song and the teachers began cleaning and folding tables. Some students helped while others chased each other around with their costumes half on, half off. The rear doors leading to the staff parking lot were open to let in some fresh air, so I stepped outside and took a deep breath. The sky was clear; the moon was big and full and bright.

"You look a little sad," a voice behind me said.

It was Miss Diamond.

"You need a friend?"

She had on a short black leather jacket and looked as though she was ready to leave. She had taken off her flip-flops and was now wearing black hiking boots.

"Sure," I said. "I think I lost mine..."

"You mean Alex?" she asked.

"Yeah, I can't seem to find her anywhere."

She was right next to me now. She closed the gym doors and said, "Maybe the Big Bad Wolf *ate her all up...*" Sexual innuendo dripped as thick as molasses.

"That's what I'm afraid of," I said nervously, as if I had never met this blond beauty. She was so different tonight. So electrically youthful. Like she was one of us; not a teacher.

"Do you need a ride home?" she asked. "It's on my way."

I felt a cold shiver run through my body. Ice down my spine.

"Ah..." I had to think for a moment, "...yeah, maybe," I said. "I was supposed to take the bus home, but—"

"With Alex?" she asked.

"No, she lives the opposite way."

"Come..." She wrapped her arm around my shoulder and guided me toward her red (of course) Honda Accord. She looked around nervously, as if making sure nobody saw us. "...I'll take you."

We pulled out of the school parking lot and made a right on Deer Lake Parkway. But then, to my surprise and confusion, instead of continuing to Royal Oak, she made a quick left on Deer Lake Avenue, and then a sharp right on Rowan and drove until she was parked right in front of a big yellow DEAD END sign.

"I love it out here," she said, turning off the car and unbuckling her seat belt. "Come on." She got out of the car.

I unclicked my belt very slowly, puzzled and unsure of what to expect.

I followed her through some thick brush to a path I had traversed many times during P.E. class. She was way ahead of me and moving in a light jog.

I finally reached the end of the trail and saw her sitting on a wooden bench in front of the lake. Well...it's called a "lake" but it's more of a swamp. It's small and shallow and filled with filthy weeds. There is a tiny sandy beach just off Sperling Avenue where one can rent boats and swim. We were on the opposite end, the area where you would encounter more geese than humans.

"Look at that moon," Miss Diamond said. "It's fucking gorgeous..."

And so are you, I wanted to say. But instead, "Yeah, it's pretty cool," was what I came up with. "Are we hangin' out here for a bit...?"

"Sit down," she said, patting the seat next to her.

I sat down on her right. She inched right up close to me and gazed at the water. She then draped her leg over mine.

Whoa...

The back of my hand on my lap was touching her outer thigh.

"Can I show you something?" she said.

I couldn't speak. I just nodded like a deaf and dumb mute.

Her eyes met mine as she took off her bomber jacket and placed it behind her. She was breathing heavily; I could tell she was nervous. Her breasts swelled.

I knew what was about to happen. I knew exactly where this was headed. I didn't know why, but I knew the outcome. *And I could have stopped it.* I could have gotten up and walked back to the car and sat down and buckled up and asked her to take me home, but instead I said "I wanna see you."

"I want you to see me, too," she replied. She slipped both bathing suit straps off her shoulders and pulled them down, exposing her breasts. Her nipples were erect. Just as I was. They were pink and filled with blood. Just as I was.

I swallowed hard and my stomach felt hollow and empty. I was suddenly cold, and I shivered a bit. I couldn't breathe. It was the first time I had ever seen a woman naked like this.

"Well...?" she said. "Do you like them?"

Pure instinct took over and I leaned into her and sucked vigorously on her left breast. I sucked like I was feeding for the first time. I licked around her areole (something I had seen in a movie somewhere) and then sucked some more. I cupped her other breast in my hand and squeezed. She moaned.

She started rubbing my penis through my costume. My hard-on was about to poke right through my futuristic uniform.

I switched breasts as she said, "Yeah, don't stop," and continued to rub me. But then I came.

I backed off her breast and looked at her. "Sorry," was all I could manage.

"You didn't do anything wrong, sweetie." She came in close and gently kissed my lips. "You did everything right," she whispered.

I was a soaked mess.

She pulled her straps back over her shoulders and looked around for witnesses.

We stood up. She held me by my shoulders. She was quite a few inches taller than I was and had to look down at me. She kissed me using her tongue. It felt as though dynamite had gone off in my mouth. I could hear fireworks and firecrackers off in the distance. Screechers and screamers popping and snapping—the usual Halloween paraphernalia.

She turned around and put her jacket back on.

"Do you think we could go back to the school?" I asked.

She looked confused. "Why?"

"I have a pair of track pants in my locker," I said. "I can't go home like this—" I pointed to my crotch.

She smirked. And then she did something that should have made me question her sanity. But when you're a teenager and a stunning, mature woman gives herself to you like this, nothing is *normal*, nothing is *sane*. Her knees made a tiny popping sound as she squatted, took an exaggerated whiff of my crotch, leaned her head back and then exhaled. "That's beautiful," she said.

As we walked back to her car I pinched myself.

It hurt.

It wasn't a dream.

"Hop in the back and duck down," she said as we pulled into the school parking lot. "Just in case there's anyone around." She bit her lip and scanned the horizon nervously. "What's your locker combo?"

I told her.

She parked the car.

There were half a dozen cars left in the lot. A few teachers and a couple of parent volunteers were still cleaning up and chatting away. It totally sucked that I had school tomorrow. I wished it was Saturday.

Miss Diamond (Do I call her Lena now? I mean, I just had her breasts in my mouth...) entered the school and turned left toward my locker.

I was lying down on the back seat and staring up at the car roof, trying to figure out what this all meant now. Where was this headed? A student teacher relationship? I'd seen and heard enough on the news that I knew it never ended well for either. But this was different. I was sixteen and she was, I think, like, thirty or something; but it was so *right*. I felt loved. Cared for. Nurtured. She wanted to be with me. And in one and a half years we could—

The car door opened.

A BULLIED REUNION

"Here," she said, breathing hard. "I found a T-shirt, too."

"Awesome, thanks," I said. Then: "Can you help me with this?" I pointed to the zipper which was at the back of the costume.

"Not here. We need to leave."

She seemed uncomfortable.

We took a right again onto Deer Lake Parkway, but this time we kept on going.

"There," she said once we were clear of the school, "that's better."

We were parked across the street from my apartment. It was a massively old, twenty-story building that cast the moon's shadow and clothed us in darkness. I was already changed. My costume was rolled up tight next to me. Miss Diamond killed the ignition and turned her head to the right, just barely looking at me from the corner of her eye. "You better go now," she said. "But I'll see you tomorrow, okay?" She seemed shy. Like she couldn't look me in the eye.

I moved forward and kissed her cheek. She did not move.

"We have to be very careful," she said.

"I want this," I said.

"So do I. But it's dangerous. For both of us—"

"Good." I wanted to show her I was man enough to handle our affection.

She turned around and faced me. Our faces almost touched. "I think you're a very special young man," she said. "And I'd like to explore everything about you…"

Flashing blue and red lights engulfed the vehicle. A police cruiser double-parked in front of my building. The officer got out. I ducked my head down and Miss Diamond froze. She was terrified as he walked toward the car.

She rolled down the window as he approached, shining his flashlight. "Are you gonna be long?" he asked. "I need the space."

"I was just leaving," she said. Her voice cracked, and she swallowed hard. It wouldn't be the worst thing in the world for a female teacher to be caught with a male student lying down in the back seat of her car with a cum-stained *Star Trek* uniform, would it?

"Thank you," the officer said.

99

Miss Diamond started the Honda and pulled out of the parking spot. The police cruiser slipped in right after her.

"I'll drop you off on the next block," she said.

I noticed her right hand was trembling on the steering wheel.

"Hey, it's okay," I said. "Relax."

I felt all manned-up now. I had this magnificent specimen that wanted to be with me. A person that was risking a lot in her life to engage in a relationship with *me*!

She let out a breath. "That was close."

The digital clock on the dashboard said it was 9:42 p.m.

My mom would be worried if I was any later. The dance ended around 9:00 p.m.

"I guess I'll see ya tomorrow," I said. I got out of the car and closed the door.

Ms. Diamond rolled down her window. "At school, when we see each other, it's Ms. Diamond. But out here—in our world—you call me Lena, okay?"

"Okay." I leaned in and kissed her hard.

"Bye," she said.

I walked up the street, the flashing lights guiding me through the darkness.

*   *   *

Whenever you see a police officer standing in your doorway it is never good news. Always dreadful. They don't come to tell you you've won the lottery, or that something great and grand was about to happen. No. Unfortunately, they are the bearers of BAD news. And so, when I got off the elevator on the eighth floor of my apartment building and saw an officer standing in our entrance, with his shoulder mic crackling away with clipped voices, my stomach fell into my knees, my heart worked its way up to my throat, and my head lost all its weight and floated above my shoulders as though it was unattached.

"What's goin' on?" I asked the officer.

A BULLIED REUNION

"Do you live here?" he asked.

"Yeah," I said, and stepped into my apartment.

He put his hand on my shoulder, but I pulled away and kept walking.

Mom was crying uncontrollably on the couch. A female cop sat next to her. I heard my grandpa screaming at the gods in Romanian in the bedroom with my grandma wailing along.

"Mom, what's wrong?!" I asked.

"Your father was involved in a very serious motor vehicle accident," a young female officer said. She was short and stocky, with black hair slicked back into a pony tail. "They did everything they could in the ambulance… unfortunately, he died on the way to the hospital. I'm very sorry."

I didn't look at her. All I could see was my mom with her face in her hands, her whole body convulsed and pulsated, "No, no, no…" was all she could say.

"We need to leave now," the officer said to me. "But a counsellor will be by in the morning to help, okay?"

I nodded my head. Totally numb.

She spoke into her shoulder mic and left the apartment with the other officer. The door slammed a little too loudly on their way out.

My mother spent the night on the couch. My grandpa didn't sleep at all. The bed squeaked from all the tossing and turning; he was moaning and swearing in Romanian at the devil and all his minions. My sister was in bed before the whole ruckus started and never heard a word of it. I slept in my parent's bed. On my mother's side.

I hadn't spilled a tear yet…

The stove clock read 8:22 a.m.

The phone rang.

It was a counsellor that worked with the local detachment. She wanted to speak with my mother.

"She's out cold on the couch," I said. "She hasn't really slept, and we should let her sleep."

"That's good," the counsellor said, "she needs it. I'll call later to check in. And you don't have to go to school today. Your family needs you. So just stay home and be with them, all right?"

"OK. Can you call the school?"

"It's already done," she replied. "They'll have some work sent to you for the week. And then we'll see how you're doing next week."

"Thank you."

When I hung up the phone I felt more alone than I ever had. And it wasn't because my father was gone—we were never that close—it was, I think, because it's all *me* now. My mother, I knew, would *never* be the same. With Mom's new job and the little lottery windfall—which she used to pay off credit card debt—my grandparents could now move to their own apartment, which would make the place almost empty.

My sister walked into the living room and saw Mom on the couch. Even at six years of age she knew that something bad had happened. "How come Mommy's on the couch?" she asked. But then Grandpa picked her up, kissed her chubby cheek, and carried her to the kitchen for a bowl of Fruit Loops.

"Are you serious?" Alex said. She called from the payphone at first break.

"Yeah, I am," I said. "Mom's gotta go to the morgue or something…I dunno."

"Fuck… You want me to come by after school?"

"Nah, it's all weird right now. Maybe tomorrow."

"Okay…look, I'm sorry about last night. I know I skipped out on you and stuff."

"I don't care." I had already forgotten about it. I had two diametrically opposed thoughts battling for supremacy in my mind: what I had done with Miss Diamond, and the sadness that had befallen my home…

"But I do—and I'm sorry. It was stupid. I ended up with this guy—"

"I really don't give a fuck," I said, a little too harshly.

The bell rang in the background.

"I gotta go," she said.

Mom walked into the kitchen as I hung up the phone. She smelled like perfume and was all done up.

She poured herself half a cup of coffee, pulled out a bottle of Sambuca from the cupboard, and filled the rest with it. She then added a dash of cream.

I was so happy and proud that she had been sober since she got the job at the bank, but I knew that was not only about to end, but most likely spiral out of control.

She took a big pull directly from the bottle, swallowed, and said, "I'll be home later." With that, she walked out the door.

A BULLIED REUNION

The bottle of Sambuca was still on the counter. I picked it up to put it away, but then something took a hold of me: a *fuck-it* feeling I had never felt before. Suddenly, I found myself unscrewing the cap and chugging the sweet mixture down. As I had never touched the stuff—a sip of beer and a shot of Romanian vodka at a New Year's Eve gathering once—I coughed and gagged. But then I took a slower swallow; a more mindful drink. The inner *warmth* came…followed by its close cousin, *calm.* My head felt as though it was made of cotton. My body felt numb and distant again, like it did the previous night. I walked in a bubble to the couch and sat down, turned on the TV—bottle still in my hand—and flipped channels for the next hour while I slowly sipped. There was nothing on except reruns of *The A-Team* and *Baywatch*. It was the one with the *Playboy* model and "Tool Time girl" from *Home Improvement*, not the season with the one who looked like Lena.

The phone woke me up from the couch. I jumped up a little too quickly and felt nauseous and dizzy. I puked into the kitchen sink, wiped my mouth on a towel that hung on the stove handle, and answered the line—

"Hello?"

The stove clock told me it was 12:31 p.m.

"Hey, it's me," said Lena.

I cleared my throat, said, "Hey." I took a seat at the kitchen table. The phone cord was long enough to reach the couch, but I felt if I didn't sit down right away I would end up retching into the sink again while the love of my life listened.

"I saw Alex in the hallway," she said. "She told me what happened."

I could tell she was holding back tears. And I could also hear a few teachers in the background gabbing about how noisy Halloween gets every year, fireworks and crackers and whatnot.

"I'd like to see you today," she whispered

"I'd like to see you, too."

A pause.

"I'll pick you up on the corner, where I dropped you off last night."

I could barely hear her. What would another teacher think if they saw her whispering into the phone?

"Yeah, that'd be good… What time?"

"I can be there at four."

"Okay…it'd be nice to talk to somebody."

"And I'd like to be that *somebody*."

The house was empty. My grandparents probably took my sister out for some fresh air since she wasn't going to kindergarten. I went back to the couch and noticed the bottle was gone. Gramps must have put it back. But when I looked in the cupboard above the stove, I saw that it was completely cleaned out. He saw the storm on the horizon and knew his daughter well.

Mom called but I didn't know where she was. (Where do you go to deal with the dead in your life?) She said she wouldn't be home for a while. She said she took a taxi but that Rodica would pick her up. And then she asked about Lucia and she wanted to talk to her, but I said I didn't have a clue where she was. "They're probably at the park," was all I could guess. My mom asked if I was okay. "Sure," I said. "That's life." She kept blowing her nose on the other end. The stove clicked its analog hand to 3:56 p.m. I told her I was heading out. That I needed to get away. (I had a weird headache I couldn't shake. Oddly enough, I knew if I had another couple of sips the sharp pain and pounding would stop.) She asked where I was going. "Just out. I dunno. I can't sit here anymore..."

The phone beeped.

"I gotta go," I said. "Someone's trying to buzz in."

"Who is it?" she said.

"I dunno, probably Grandpa. Maybe he forgot his keys."

She kissed me goodbye through the phone and hung up.

We had one of those phones where the dial pad was right inside the receiver. So I clicked the button near the earpiece that would kill the line and held my finger there for just a second until I heard the buzzing again. I lifted my finger off the button and put the phone to my ear to switch lines. "Hello?"

"I'm downstairs," Alex said. (Like, where else would she be if she was talking to me through this damn thing.)

I was angry. Why was she here?! I had to go!

"Whattya doin' here?" I asked.

"I just thought you needed a friend." She could tell I was caught off guard but wasn't sure why I was dismissing her. "I can go if you want..."

"I'm kinda busy right now. I'm leaving."

"Okay—I can take a hint." She hung up. And I felt like a total asshole.

I pushed "9" and heard the static of life outside downstairs. "Alex—hey, Alex!" I called out through the line. I wanted to apologize, but there was no answer. She was gone.

* * *

I had on my cleanest, crispest pair of Levi's, and my white Adidas indoor soccer shoes. A white Umbro T-shirt with a black Umbro track jacket completed the *I am a soccer fanatic* ensemble. The sun was bright in the sky and a moist decay permeated the air. Even though death was at my door, I had never felt more alive. A pure sense of freedom engulfed me. It was as though I had gained something rather than lost. Like a weight was lifted off my life. As though maybe I could finally become the person I was supposed to be. The one that was going to guide me through that transition sat in her little red four-door Accord, waving and smiling and glowing, full of life and promise. Energy sent blood rushing to my head, eradicating any imbalances and impurities.

I felt confident and powerful. *Fuck everyone and everything.* I bent through the open window and kissed her on the mouth. She held my face for a moment.

"I fucking love you," she said. I smiled and she drew my face to hers, tilted my head, and whispered into my ear, "Soon I'll say: 'I love fucking you'."

Unbeknownst to me, Alex was watching from behind the bushes of my apartment. She had waited to see where I was going.

I slipped into the front seat as Lena—ah, yes, for today it would be Lena, not Miss Diamond—turned the ignition and we sped away. The Accord disappeared in a purring whirlwind of excitement and sexual tension.

First stop: Lena's apartment.

We had to get the obvious out of the way. We couldn't continue with our relationship in this unconsummated state.

CHRIS PONICI

"Here, hold this for a sec," Lena said, handing me her purse while she messed with the door. She was clearly nervous. She didn't want anybody to see her in the underground garage fiddling with the lock while one of her students held her purse. We looked as obvious as a prom couple stopping off at Shoppers Drug Mart before the big night: everyone knew what was about to go down…(pun completely and totally intended).

The knob finally turned, and we scurried to the elevator. She pushed the button that would take us up to the tenth floor. Her building was less than a twenty minute walk from mine.

"Here we are…" she said, closing her door.

Her apartment was barely furnished. The carpets were old and brown and kind of gross. Her kitchen table was full of bills and old plates from the day before. The sink was a nightmare. Her television was a TV/VCR combo and was no bigger than 15". And all she had to sit on was one La-Z-Boy recliner parked six feet away from the screen.

"Sorry about the mess," she said. Then she came in close. She was not a reflection of her surroundings. She was flawlessly clean and smelled like shampoo and soap and hand cream and perfection every time I was near her.

She kissed me and took off my jacket. She grabbed the bottom of my shirt and pulled it up over my head and got down on her knees and kissed and licked my abs. I felt my zipper come undone. She took me into her mouth. She sucked slow and long, and moaned a little each time she drew me in deep. (I was worried I would go off right away, but I was actually a little numb down there; it must have been the alcohol from earlier.)

She took off her top and unstrapped her bra. Her breasts bounced and wiggled a little when she snapped it off and threw it on the ground next to her. She looked up at me with her doe eyes. "Let's go to the bedroom." She stood up and took my hand in hers.

And, yes, indeed, this was a room with a bed—a mattress, that is, on the floor…no actual "bed" to speak of—and a tiny brown dresser with a small mirror (no frame) stuck (yes, stuck) to the wall.

She slipped off her blue jeans and then fell back on the mattress with nothing but her pink lace panties on.

"Come," she said.

And I did.

Violently. I pounded her body until I exploded and my entire being shuttered and shook, as though I was electrocuted with my cock in her socket. She left the room cupping her vagina. The toilet flushed as I laid back and stared at the ceiling. The greatest moment of my life had taken place within twenty-four hours of my father's death. That's how life works sometimes.

"That was quite the ride," she said, standing naked in the doorway. She held a bottle of tequila in one hand and two shot glasses in the other. The bedroom blinds were wide open, and the sun worshiped her body. She glistened in the light; her swimmer's legs and flat stomach were sweaty and shiny, her nipples pointed straight out: pink and perky. She slid under the blankets next to me, handed me a glass, and poured it right to the rim, then repeated for herself.

"Here's to us...forever."

It sounded like a wedding toast. She threw the shot back. I followed accordingly and almost gagged, but I kept a straight face. It was not as sweet and easy as Sambuca; more bite with a killer aftertaste. She refilled our glasses and we downed them.

I was warm.

I was happy.

I was horny and ready again.

This time I took a little longer. I wanted the ecstasy to last. To never end...

*   *   *

We lay beside each other, naked and spent. She stroked my stomach with her head on my chest and said nothing. We said and did everything that was needed to be said and done.

It was dark outside when I next opened my eyes. The green numbers on the digital clock on the floor next to me were blurry and I couldn't see the time. I was alone in Lena's room; it smelled like sex and sweat. The heat was blowing through the vents and I felt a little dizzy. I couldn't remember how many tequila shots we had before copulating like wild chimpanzees.

I heard the TV: canned laughter and a clap-track. I grabbed my clothes and put them on in the wrong order. I couldn't find my underwear, so I went commando. Lena was in her La-Z-Boy watching reruns of *I Love Lucy*. She was wrapped in a furry blanket that looked like an animal pelt.

"What time is it?" I asked.

"Come here," she said. She kissed me as I bent down. "It's a little after eight."

"Fuck. My mom's probably wondering where I am," I said.

"I'm really sorry about your dad." She hit the mute button. But it was suddenly too quiet.

"It is what it is…" I shrugged my shoulders, hands in pockets. "We were never really that close."

"But he was still your father—I'm sure it hurts."

"Yeah, sort of." I wanted to go back in the room with her and try for round three, but I could tell by the way she looked at me that it was time I left.

We kissed passionately for a few seconds—what kids would call "sucked face"—in her Accord a block away from my place.

"I guess you'll take some time off school?" she asked.

All I wanted to do was to stay with her. To go back to her place and never leave. "Yeah, probably the rest of the week," I said.

"I'm at the pool tomorrow night—and Friday," she said, "but we'll see each other Saturday, okay?"

I nodded and kissed her goodbye.

She blew me a kiss and flashed her lights at me as she drove away.

* * *

"Where were you?!" my mom literally screamed at me as I walked in the front door. "I was worried sick!"

"I went out with some friends…sorry," I said.

My entire broken family was in the living room. Grandpa was standing next to the balcony door, staring out the window. Grandma was on the couch with my baby sister, reading her a book. Mom paced around nervously, her fists clenched.

"Do you know how much it is going to cost to bury your father?" she asked. Her face was red from crying, her eyes were distant, unfocused, and aimlessly scanned the room, as if the answer to her misery was stuck on one of our walls. "We have to cremate him. We can't afford anything more." She sniffled and choked up.

"We'll do whatever…it's okay," I said. I wrapped my arm around her shoulder and I leaned into her. She was taller than me, so her cheek rested on top of my head.

Grandpa piped up. "He was a drunken fool," he said in Romanian. "Idiot."

I had not heard any of the details of the accident. But I think I know what he was hinting at.

"Was Dad drinking?" I asked Mom.

She pulled away and went into her bedroom. Her sobs followed closely.

"He was driving drunk," Grandpa said. He sat on a chair next to the window and looked right at me. "He went straight through the windshield. They found him on the pavement. His head was cracked in half. We're lucky he didn't kill anyone."

Grandpa was a World War II veteran who never pulled any punches or sugar-coated anything.

I swallowed hard. "Mom's a mess," I said.

"How about you," he asked. "You okay?"

"Yeah, I guess."

Grandma finished the book and put it down on the coffee table. My sister knew something happened and that Dad wouldn't be coming home anymore. She was trying to process it and seemed very distant. No smile. No emotion. Fucking tough on a six-year-old.

"Let's get you to bed," Grandma said as she picked her up and whisked her out of the living room.

It was just me and Gramps. I sat on the far end of the couch. "Where were you today?" he asked. "After you drank your face off."

I remembered how I was passed out on the couch and then saw the liquor cabinet was emptied out. "I was with a friend."

*   *   *

Miss Diamond dropped off a week's worth of homework for each class on Friday after school. She said hello to Mom and offered her condolences. She gave me a knowing look and then left. I wanted to go to the aquatic centre and see her but I knew we already had plans on Saturday. Also, I didn't want anybody to see me swimming and happy right after my dad kicked life's bucket. That would be completely inappropriate.

The apartment, strangely enough, felt smaller after my father died. It was like we were constantly in each other's way. We bumped into one another and tried to cook just as someone else was doing the same. Suddenly, one TV wasn't enough so Mom bought one for my grandparent's bedroom (they decided not to move out until Mom figured out all her shit).

"I'm going to put you and your sister in my room," Mom said. We were sitting at the kitchen table. I was reading my chemistry textbook and she was having a cup of decaf. "And I'll take the sofa. I'll get you a bunk-bed on the weekend."

I wondered how many other grade elevens had to endure sleeping in the same room as their six-year-old sister…

"Yeah, that's cool," I said. No need to make a big deal out of it.

The phone rang and I picked up. It was Alex. She wanted to know what I was up to; if I wanted to sleep over and then hang out tomorrow. I told her I couldn't. And when she asked me why, I didn't have an answer. If I told her the truth—I was going to Miss Diamond's apartment where I would suck and fuck every inch of her body until she begged me to stop—she either wouldn't believe me or she would try to stop me. And if I lied, she'd probably catch me.   "Seriously," Alex said, "like, what are you doing that we can't hang out?" she pressed.

"I'm just busy doing stuff for my mom," I said.

"Does your mom drive a red Honda Accord?"

Oh, fuck…

"What?" I said.

"Does your mom drive a Honda Accord?" she asked again.

"How do you know?" I asked. "How the fuck do you—?" Mom looked at me with curious eyes.

"I saw you," Alex said.

I could not continue this conversation here, in front of my mother. "I can't talk right now," I said. But that was completely obvious. And now my mom really looked at me. A *what-the-heck-is-going-on* scowl suddenly made an appearance on her face.

"Whatever. I don't care. Fuck up your life," Alex warned.

I wanted her to shut up. I wanted her to stop talking about it. Alex hung up without another word. Great. My best friend was now pissed at me.

"What was that about?" my mom asked.

"Nothing," I said. "Just high school bullshit."

"Just wait until you're an adult," she said. "Then it really begins..."

Truth was, I already felt like one.

She put her empty mug in the sink and went over to the couch.

"Hey, Mom," I said. "Alex wanted me to sleep over. Can I go?"

Flipping through channels, she nodded. "But you have to take the bus, I'm not driving you."

"Thanks," I said. And went off to my room to pack an overnight bag.

The pay phone in our lobby always had a quarter in the slot. It's like half the people in this place forgot that if your call does not go through you do get your twenty-five cents back! I scooped out the quarter, threw it into the slot, and dialed the aquatic centre. (I found the number in the phone book that was chained to the small desk underneath.)

"Hi, can I please speak to Miss Lena Diamond? I think she's working tonight."

"She is," a sweet twenty-something voice said on the other end of the line, "but she's at her post. Can I take a message?"

"Actually, this is quite urgent. I'm on the student council and we have to move our meeting to tomorrow instead of Monday. Do you think I could hold the line while you go get her?" A maturity arose in my voice that had not been there before. (Virginity lost. Manhood gained.) Sometimes in life you have to give direction instead of asking for something. Tell those around you what you need them to do and they will do it. Ask with confidence and purpose and things get done.

"Um...yeah, hold on a minute," she said.

I held the line for what seemed to be a very long minute—more like five. Local rock sensation Bryan Adams' "All for Love" was followed by Ace Of Base with "The Sign."

"Hello?" Lena's voice came through the phone—cutting off the music.

"Hey, it's me," I said.

"Cris?" she said. "What are you doing? Is everything okay?"

She sounded more like my mother than my lover.

"Yeah, of course. I wanna come over tonight. I got my stuff. And my mom thinks I'm at a friend's house."

I could hear her clear her throat and I imagined there were probably staff and customers all around her, making this exchange quite awkward.

I said, "It's okay, I told your gal there I was on the student council. Just say 'Yes, we can change the date, no problem' and I'll hop on a bus and come right over."

"Yes, we can change the date, no problem," she said.

"Good. I'll see you when you're done." She had taped her apartment key into one of my binders that she dropped off. She knew my locker combo and I had the key to her home. And her heart.

I was on my way.

*   *   *

We fucked. And then we fucked again. And then we woke up around two in the morning and went at it one more time.

I was raw. Sore. Spent.

For the next week that's all we really did. Mom thought I was hanging out with Alex—I told her I really needed a friend right now—after school. Lena would pick me up a couple of blocks away and we would drive somewhere secluded and fuck in the backseat, depending on what mood she was in.

I couldn't get enough of her. As *hard* as I tried, I could not satiate myself. It was as if the more time I spent with her, the more I wanted her. (One night she bought a bottle of champagne and I poured it all over her body and slurped it off her while we sat in her tub. On another night she brought home whipped cream and, well, you know, we did all those clichéd bedroom things...)

She told me a friend of hers had a cabin up at Whistler and she wanted to spend a weekend with me there. I told her it would be difficult to get away for that long, and that it might be a little too public. We should wait until I graduate, then it wouldn't matter. She agreed, but I could tell she really wanted to go.

On the weekend before I was supposed to head back to school after a little over a week off (and before my dad's memorial service on Sunday), our secret love nearly came to light.

"Alex called asking for you," Mom said as I walked in the door. It was ten o'clock sharp and I had just returned from Lena's Love Cavern.

I swallowed hard and tried to stall. "Who?" I said.

She furiously flipped through a *Chatelaine* magazine on the couch and said, "Alex, your friend. And what do you think I told her?" She had yet to look at me.

"I don't know what you told her, Mom. I'm tired. And I'm goin' to bed."

"She's a very good friend," my mother said. "She tried to cover for you. Said something about not being able to make it to the movies tonight. But you weren't going to the movies. You told me you were going to her house for dinner and then to the pool. You even brought your shorts."

I could not move. I stood frozen in the hallway, trying to figure a way out of this. I could not pause for too long otherwise she would know that I was lying.

"Well, we were *supposed* to go to the movies—I mean, swimming, but then"—fuck, I sucked at lying—"but then she changed her mind, so we went to the movies, but she couldn't make it, and—" She wasn't buying it, and, quite frankly, neither was I.

She closed the magazine, threw it on the coffee table. "Why?"

I was in the living room now, next to her on the couch, standing firm, trying to muster up some courage and confidence. "There's things I do that are private."

"Private?" she said. "You don't have *private* things in my house! I am your mother!" She stood tall and straight now, her eyes directly on me. "And I don't need this shit!"

I felt horrible. I wanted to calm her down, settle her suspicions. "Mom," I said as I hugged her tight, "I'll tell you, but not right now, all right? I'm safe. I'm okay. I was with another friend. Alex doesn't know... It's hard to explain."

Maybe because she was exhausted or she'd had enough or she actually trusted me and didn't want to take this any further, she just said, "Okay," and left it at that.

I sighed in relief and let her go.

I looked her in the eyes and said, "We say goodbye to Dad tomorrow. Let's focus on that."

"What am I going to do?" she said. She began to cry, pushed past me and went into the bathroom. She sobbed and hit the counter with her fist.

I picked up the phone in the kitchen and dialed Alex's number. I had to tell her the truth.

* * *

I stood in the front row of the church next to Alex and the rest of my family. We looked at my father's urn. All I could think of was how everything that was left of him was in that little golden chalice-type thing; it looked like something out of an *Indiana Jones* movie. It was like it held some great secret or magic elixir—something that would turn back time if you drank it. It could have held a treasure map or maybe it was a priceless artifact made in Mesopotamia that contained the remains of a great Assyrian warrior. But no, it was just my dad: an alcoholic, un-employed Romanian chemist who escaped a communist country to give his family a better life, but who could not save himself from the dictatorship of addiction.

Alex placed her hand around my shoulder as the priest began his liturgy. The repetitive Romanian chanting and praying and blessing of the dead from the priest in his deep bass voice was soothing. He asked for God to forgive my father for all his sins as well as ours and I wondered if it was too late for that. He made the sign of the cross about a hundred times, lifted both hands to heaven and asked for God's light and love and peace to shine upon our family. But I could see right through this whole façade. The man did not put his heart into what he was saying; he looked completely detached. And I knew it was because my mother had my father cremated, a practice that's frowned upon by the Orthodox Church. *How can the dead in Christ rise on that glorious day when He shall return triumphant to gather His people if they are dust and not buried in body?* But my parents were about as un-religious as you could get without being full-blown heathens. Christmas and Easter were the only time I ever set foot inside the walls of a cathedral. Had the church not been struggling financially, I am sure they would have rejected this booking. But money talks…and so, the holy water was sprinkled, and priests prayed and performed the rituals to placate my mother and collect a fee for services rendered.

"It smells bad in here," Alex whispered. And it did. The incense that burned carried the odor of stale cheese inside old socks. "Gross."

The stained glass windows that depicted Jesus' birth, death, and resurrection let in rays of light that cut through the centre of the church and glared off my father's urn. It was as if heaven's spotlight was on him for the next hour. The golden cross with a naked Lord bleeding and crying out in agony hung behind the priest. It shook every time an eighteen-wheeler drove by outside. The hard, wooden pews hurt my ass and back; they cracked and squeaked as Alex shifted constantly next to me.

"All rise," the priest commanded in Romanian. He then asked us to repeat a prayer and blessed us for the last time. Then he walked behind a curtain like some ancient magician or great wizard who only appeared before the people when summoned.

It was a cold and abrupt end. Nobody was quite sure what to do. The priest was surely not going to touch the urn and since there was no burial, his job was done. An uncomfortable silence prevailed for the next few minutes, until my grandfather walked up to the front and picked up my father's new dwelling and carried it with him down the aisle. We all instinctively followed. He led us downstairs, into the deep basement, where there was a small room with tables and some food spread out. He placed my father at the head of the table, right next to a big bowl of *Koliva*, the traditional Orthodox food made of boiled wheat, raisins, and walnuts and asked us all to partake in one final meal.

"It looks like chip dip," Alex said when she saw the offering.

Although I found this to be a little morbid and completely weird, I was hungry, so I ate. There were finger foods, desserts, and self-serve bottles of wine. Some of my dad's former colleagues, a bunch of Romanians he knew from "the old country" he spent time with every so often, and mostly my mom's and grandfather's close friends were in attendance. About twenty people in all.

Sergiu Vasilescu, who most considered to be my dad's best friend, was in the car when they crashed. He poured Tuica—a type of Romanian moonshine—into shot glasses for everyone (even for Alex and me—underage drinking was no big thing in the Romanian community), and then he raised his glass and asked everyone to do so as well.

"To my dear friend, Radu Leuca," he said in broken English as he looked up at the ceiling and tried to hone in on heaven's coordinates. "We miss you and we love you. And your family is our family." He looked over at my mother. "And we take care of our own…" Everyone raised their glasses a little higher in a *salut!* and downed the shot.

Alex coughed hard. I could handle it, no problem. I was used to it. Lena and I drank vodka straight from the bottle before *and* after sex.

"Another round?" I asked Alex.

"No, thanks," she replied. "I'm good."

As people around me ate and talked and laughed and told stories about my father, my mother came up to me—in her matter-of-fact way—and said, "I am going to work tomorrow, and you are going to school. And we move on from this." She looked as though her strength had come back. She did not seem as despondent or worried anymore. It was as if someone had given her some sort of reassurance.

"Yeah, I know," I said to her. And then she wrapped her arms around both Alex and I and squeezed us tight. Each one of our heads were against her shoulders.

*   *   *

Christmas and New Year's came and went without a whole lot of fanfare. Mom was doing well. She worked full-time, went shopping with friends, and bought new clothes. She spent money on things I felt may have been a little extravagant, like a big screen TV and a brand-new entertainment centre that made our tiny living room look even smaller. On Valentine's Day, as she was getting ready to go on a date with Sergiu Vasilescu, I said, "Aren't you moving a little fast?" He seemed to leech onto her the moment my dad's body and life was reduced to ashes. One time, I heard Grandpa yelling in Romanian about "life insurance" and how that money was supposed to be for "the kids' education" and how she was "pissing away our future," or what little of it we had. I didn't really understand all of it, but I got the drift: Mom came into a cash windfall and was using the money to anodyne herself.

But I guess I was happy for her. Because I was happy for myself. I was meeting Lena on the corner at seven o'clock and we were going out to a restaurant. It was a little risky, but it was supposed to be at some expensive Italian place in Gastown.

"No teacher or student will be there," Lena said. "It's way too expensive."

So, I told Mom I was going out with Alex and some friends. Alex knew by then that I used her as a cover; she didn't care as long as I forewarned her. I put on the same suit and tie Mom bought for my father's memorial service, slicked my hair back nicely, sprayed some cologne on my neck, and walked out the door, ready to meet my love, my life, my *teacher*, my Valentine.

Umberto's was located in the centre of the famous tourist attraction known as Gastown, the heart of downtown Vancouver. It was right along the waterfront near the ports and massive hotels and convention centres that were frequented by both billionaire businessmen and rich celebrities. The brick buildings that lined Water Street looked like New York tenements—like something out of an old mafia movie. Lena parked the car a block away from the restaurant and we actually walked onto a movie set! Filming had stopped for the day, but we saw generators covered in tarps, huge overhead spotlights and lamps, compressors, and a few railway tracks the cameras would run along while filming chase scenes and whatnot. A couple of heavy-set security guards patrolled the area in their bright yellow jackets and red and blue turbans.

"Good evening. Welcome to Umberto's," the maître d' said as I held the front door for the very lovely Ms. Lena Diamond. The strapping young Italian led us to our table that was nestled in a quiet corner of the restaurant, right in front of the massive floor-to-ceiling windows that displayed Vancouver's glorious North Shore. He pulled Lena's chair out and waited for her to be seated, but not before he caught a glimpse of her splendid thighs as she sat down. She wore a form-fitted, cherry red, sleeveless dress, and a thick gold necklace with the head of a lion as a pendant on the end. She carried a matching red clutch with a golden handle and the same lion's head on both sides. She was perfectly put together and devilishly sexy.

"Enjoy your evening," he said.

She tapped my leg underneath the table with her high heels. "Isn't this fantastic?"

Taken literally, yes, this evening was extraordinarily fantastic! Dating the hottest teacher in the school—nay, the hottest in the entire *district*—was completely unlikely. But it was happening...and it was happening to me!

"It's pretty great," I said as I checked out the view...of her superb cleavage, which seemed to be getting fuller and fuller each and every time I saw her.

"You look really handsome tonight," she said. She noticed me checking her out, so she rubbed her finger across the top of her breasts and smiled.

I looked around the restaurant just to make sure we didn't know anybody. So far, so good.

Moments later our waiter showed up with menus and water. "Can I recommend a white wine to start?" he asked, looking at me a little suspiciously.

"No, thank you," Lena said.

The waiter removed the wine menu from the table and started to rattle off a couple of special dishes the chef had prepared for this Valentine's Day. He had a thick accent and at times it was hard to make out what he was saying, but Lena nodded and agreed. He seemed much more interested in her than me.

"I will let you take few moments for a decision and then I coming back, okay for you?" he said.

We nodded and smiled.

"I think he's French, not Italian," Lena said.

"And I think you're beautiful," I said, looking deep into her eyes. My heart relished every second we were together. She blushed and her eyes sparkled. Yes, they twinkled in the candlelight. "I have a surprise for you...but you have to wait until dessert to find out what it is," she said.

A BULLIED REUNION

We slurped our pasta like children and laughed. We didn't care, we were *in* love. Yes. Love is a place. A place you go where everything seems right and beautiful and perfect and blissful and magnificently superb; a brilliantly breathtaking dwelling on an island of complete and absolute happiness where the warmth of passion and the embrace of obsession are eternally yours. She threw her head back and laughed a full belly laugh at all my jokes. Everything about her was sexy. Not a millimetre was out of place…

Tiramisu and espresso were on their way, our waiter—who we found out was originally from Milan but moved to Montreal when he was only 12—informed us. As Pavarotti's "Caruso" played from unseen speakers, Lena said to me, "I can't wait any longer. I have to tell you."

I wiped my mouth with the cloth napkin that was on my lap. "Okay, what is it?" I was a little nervous because she sat up straight and cleared her throat like she was about to give quite the speech.

"Well…I don't know where to start," she said.

"Just say it." I was both impatient and excited.

"I'm pregnant."

"What?"

"I'm pregnant."

The waiter suddenly appeared and lowered two small plates of Tiramisu and two doppio espressos on the table. "Enjoy!" he said and sped away.

"Are you serious," I asked.

"Aren't' you happy?" she replied.

There was a crack in our foundation. This was the first time we had ever experienced tension. I didn't like it. I squirmed in my seat.

"I think it's great…" I lied. Even though I had just eaten enough bread and pasta to feed a small village for a week, my stomach felt hollow.

And then the crack doubled in size. The foundation fucking ripped open and fell apart—

"What. Are. You. Doing. Here?"

The voice was an accented staccato from directly behind me. I looked at Lena and her jaw literally dropped an inch. She looked back at me in horror.

I turned around in my seat.

It was my mother.

Sergiu was on her right.

Mom looked at me and then at Lena, who I felt in the presence of my mother instantly became *Miss Diamond*.

"I can explain everything," Miss Diamond said.

"Why are you on a date with my son?!" she said. Her arms were crossed and she leaned in close to Miss Diamond.

"It's not a date—" Miss Diamond said.

"Are you some kind of sicko?" Mom was visibly shaken.

"Honey, you need to relax," Sergiu said in Romanian. He then looked at me. "Let's go outside and talk."

"No," I replied in English. "We're not done. We can talk later. Not here."

"Are you kidding me? Are you out of your mind?" my mother said.

"Iz dare a problem?" our waiter said. "Can I help you to your seat?"

This fucking guy had no clue.

"We're leaving," my mother said to the waiter. "And so is my son and his *school teacher*." She said the last part like it was a swear word.

The surrounding patrons all stopped eating and took in the live show.

"Mom, just go away!" I shouted. Now the whole place was staring at us.

"Good evening, everyone," said the restaurant manager as he approached. "I'm afraid you must take your seats, please. You're disturbing the others." Although he carried an accent, his English was perfectly polished.

"Mom, just go sit down," I said, very calm but stern. "PLEASE."

She bit her lip and grabbed Sergiu by the arm. But instead of taking a seat, she walked out the front door. I saw she wiped her eyes with the back of her hand as the door closed behind her.

"I'm sorry about all this," Lena said to the manager (she became Lena the moment my mother left).

"No problem," the manager replied. "Enjoy your dessert." He then left.

The waiter was about to follow, but then I took a deep breath and said, "I think we should go, too."

"Very good, sir," he replied. "I bring for you the final bill."

Lena looked pale, like she had just jumped into a vat of milk. She, of course, had the most to lose in all of this. Her life. Her career. Her everything.

"What are we gonna do?" I asked.

"We have to go and talk to your mother. She can't say anything to anybody. Do you understand?" She was angry at me; almost indignant.

A BULLIED REUNION

"She won't say anything. She's not like that. She won't fuck up your life."

"I've already done that myself," Lena said. She had not looked at me since my mother came on the scene. She talked to her plate, her hands, her purse, but never once looked in my direction. It was as if we were both naked and exposed now.

I tried to reconnect. "Hey," I said, "come on. This is nothing. My mom's cool. It'll be fine." But I don't think I believed what I said myself…

When she finally looked at me she became Miss Diamond again. She said, "I'm pregnant. And the father is my sixteen-year-old student. This is not *nothing*; this is *everything*."

"And here you are," the waiter said as he placed a leather folder that contained our bill on the table. "We hope to see you again soon."

*　　*　　*

She didn't bother parking a block or two away. There was no point now. The pussy cat was out of the bag and all we had now was the truth. The bright light of honesty illuminated the facts but darkened our emotions; they scurried away like mice.

"I'll have an abortion. And then this'll all be over," Miss Diamond said.

A breathless pause held us still.

"I'm sorry I did this to you," she went on. A tear drop hit her bare thigh, and all I could think of was kissing it away. Feeling her skin on my lips. Tasting her. "I'll fix it. It'll be like it never happened."

"But that's not what I want," I said, and could barely contain my own tears. "I love you."

"I know you do," she said. "And I love you too. But that's not enough. And it's wrong."

"How can love be wrong?" I asked. "It can't. Love is *always* right. *This* is right."

She put her hand on the back of my neck and looked away, out her window, into the starry, clear night. "I have to go away."

My throat tightened. This was it and I fucking knew it. She had already made up her mind, and there was nothing I could do to stop her…

CHRIS PONICI

"Please…I don't want you to go away…" I begged. One last Hail Mary. "I'll do anything. Anything."

She looked at me and swallowed hard. "When I saw your mother tonight, I saw everything... You're a student—and I'm your teacher. This can't work. This won't work. And it has to end. You have to go upstairs and tell your mother it's over. And tomorrow I'll ask for a transfer."

This couldn't be happening, I thought. Not now. Not after all we've—

"You need to leave now," she interrupted, as if she could hear my thoughts.

"Please. Don't—"

"Now, Cris. Now…" she said sternly like a teacher, not a (past) lover.

I nodded. It was over. There was no use in trying anymore. She was done. She had made up her mind.

I got out of the car, slammed the door shut. She sped off like she couldn't get away from me fast enough.

And then she was—gone.

*   *   *

"Break it off or I'm calling the school and she *will* be fired. And probably charged, too." Mom said even before I had closed the front door. She was on the couch with Sergiu, who looked like he was already four to five beers in. Mom dangled a glass of wine in her hand and was speaking into it as if it were her microphone.

"It's already done," I said. "It's over." I stood in the middle of the living room.

"Good…good. Now go to bed," she said.

"Not until you promise me something." I walked right up to her and Sergiu. "I don't want anybody finding out. This is over. And I mean OVER." I enunciated the word the best I could. "We don't talk about it, you don't call the school, you don't mention it ever again. Ever."

She knew I was serious. She looked at Sergiu—

"Don't look at him—look at me," I said. "It's over."

My mother had never seen this side of me before: strong, confident, unyielding.

Lena had changed me into a new man, whether she knew it or not. I had just lost the love of my life and my heart was broken into a quadzillion pieces. The last thing I needed was more drama at school.

"Okay," she agreed, "it's over."

*   *   *

Miss Diamond called in sick for the rest of the week. After that she took a leave of absence until a spot opened at another school. I heard everything from Alex. She was really close to her English 11 teacher, who knew a few details of Miss Diamond's departure and whereabouts.

Life went on. Spring break, final exams, and then all of a sudden, we were on the cusp of summer. My last break before Grade 12.

Just as the temperature rose, and my memory of Miss Diamond began to fade, I heard the unthinkable. I was in bed reading the latest copy of *World Soccer* when the phone rang.

"She moved," Alex said right off the bat. Not a "Hello," or "How're you doing?" just "She's gone."

"What? Who?" I said. But I knew who she meant.

Alex took a long pause before she began. "I finished writing my English exam and hung back to say goodbye to Mrs. Hawkins for the summer," she said. "I asked if she had heard anything about Miss Diamond—'cause I knew you wanted an update—and she told me… She said she moved back to Abbotsford. I guess that's where she's from…"

I couldn't fucking believe it. What the fuck, Lena? The phone trembled in my hand. "Whatever," I said, my voice cracking. "Good for her."

"Yeah, well, the next part's a little fucked up. Mrs. Hawkins also said that Abbotsford's a better place for her to raise her baby. Her mom lives there so she'll have a lot of help."

"She's still pregnant? I thought—"

"She never had the abortion—she's keepin' the kid."

"That's my—"

"I know," Alex said. "That's why it's so fucked up. She has no right to do what she's doing. But it's not like she can just come out and say that you're the dad, right?"

I didn't know what to think.

"Alex," I said, my mind running in a million different places, "why is she keeping the baby? What does that mean?"

She didn't answer right away. Probably because she was just as confused as I was. "I don't have that answer, Cris," she said. "I really don't know. It's over my head."

The clock on my night stand read 1:45 p.m. I wanted to get off this topic. There was nothing I could do or say to change anything. I had to move on quickly. I said, "So are you all done your exams?"

"Yup—all finished," Alex replied.

"When does your Junior Police Academy start?"

"Next week—and it runs till the first week in August, I think."

"So, you'll be busy pretty much all summer?"

"Yeah, almost…it's the first year the VPD's doing it, so it should be good. My mom had to sign a consent form for the one-night ride-along at the end. That'll be fuckin' cool."

I wanted to be happy for Alex. And I was. I just couldn't express myself because I knew I would—without a doubt—never see the love of my life again.

"You wanna come over and watch a movie?" Alex asked.

"Yeah, sure." I said. "I gotta Biology exam tomorrow, but it's not till the afternoon. And I pretty much studied all day."

"I rented *From Dusk till Dawn*. It just came out. Looks all right…"

"I love Tarantino… *Pulp Fiction* was, like, one of my favourite movies."

"What about that one where they're all in that room—"

"*Reservoir Dogs*…classic."

"I only saw it once. My dad really liked it."

I felt like a kid again; movie talk and actors and just fun. No serious pregnant teacher baby shit.

"Okay, hurry up, get over here."

I hung up the phone, put on my black Umbro shorts and a Wu-Tang T-shirt with the logo on the front—that looked like some sort of bird of prey, like the Batman symbol on massive doses of steroids—and AIN'T NUTHIN' TO FUCK WIT on the back, and told my mother I would be home later.

Alex had moved to a new apartment ten stops away a couple of months before. It was a complex not unlike mine, just south of Edmonds Street, on Kingsway Avenue. She buzzed me in and I took the stairs instead of the elevator (some old lady had pushed the button and was waiting for it to arrive; she smelled like pee and old newspapers).

The front door was propped open with a shoe, so I just walked in, closed the door, and made my way to her room. She was on her bed, her small TV/VCR combo was on top of her dresser. She flipped through channels and sipped from a bottle of vodka.

"Want some?" she asked as I sat next to her on the bed. She wore a pair of grey sweatpants and a crop top with a picture of a strawberry that someone had already taken a bite out of. "I got 7-Up in the fridge if you need to mix."

"Okay," I said, and headed back to the kitchen.

"And grab some more ice," she yelled.

I returned with a bowl full of ice, two glasses, and a two litre 7-Up bottle that was almost half done.

"Here," Alex said, pouring almost half a glass of vodka.

"Holy shit!" I said. "Whattya tryin' to do, kill me?"

"Settle down," she said, dropping three ice cubes and the fizzy soda into the glass until it was full. "Chug that till it's half done."

I slammed it back in three big swallows. She then filled it right to the top again. "Now, *sip* that. You'll feel better..."

I did. The warmth of the alcohol and the rush of sugar kept me calm yet alert at the same time.

She propped another pillow up on the bed and said, "Ready?"

"Let's do it."

She pressed play and I sat back and watched...

I refilled my glass from time to time with equal parts 7-Up and vodka. An unshakable smile appeared on my face. Alex noticed and giggled. "You look like a goof," she said. "You're so fucking drunk..." Salma Hayek danced seductively on a stripper's stage as (what looked like) an albino python slithered around her half-naked body. "She's so fucking hot," Alex slurred. "I'd totally lick every inch of her body..."

"You're so fucked up," I said. The room spun. Salma poured whiskey down the front of her leg and off her foot right into Tarantino's mouth. It was an obvious salute to his massive foot fetish.

"I'm horny," Alex said. She removed her top and sat straight up on the bed. "Let's fuck."

"What are you talking about?" I said. "You're drunk...and best friends don't fuck, by the way...put your shirt on."

"It won't mean anything. Come on..."

"Alex—you're creepin' me out."

She paused the movie—just as Clooney clapped enthusiastically in response to the performance he just witnessed—and sat there in front of me. Her bare breasts, which I saw for the first time, perked-out plump and perfect.

"Come on, do me like you did that whore teacher," she said.

The alcohol really started to hit me now. I felt loose and light. My head was warm and my body felt like butter, soft and pliable. I leaned back against the pillow. "Just push PLAY," was all I could manage.

Alex then turned and puked on her bedroom floor. She was already drunk when I arrived almost an hour ago, and now she was absolutely trashed. It was mostly vodka and pop, though. It didn't look like she had eaten anything. She was so thin her stomach was inverted.

I stumbled—walking was a bit of a challenge—to the kitchen and got some paper towels. I soaked all the liquid off the carpet. Alex had passed out, topless. I covered her up with the bed sheet, kissed her forehead, and finished cleaning up. And then I watched Clooney, Tarantino, and Keitel kick vampire ass. They shot and stabbed and punched and killed their way out of that bar and rode off into the sunset. It was another Hollywood happy ending where the good guys win and the bad bullies lose—and die...

CHAPTER 6:

Twenty Year High School Reunion (2017)

I could walk right up and put a bullet in each one of their heads. Jeremy Freemont: DEAD. Robert Gregory Cook: DEAD. Michael Underwood: DEAD.

BANG! BANG! BANG! FUCK YOU—MOTHERFUCKERS!!!

But that would be too loud, too public, too easy, and too merciful for them.

No. They must suffer. They must pay. They must feel what I have felt; taste what I have tasted: pain and torment, blood and bile.

If the past ten years of practicing law had taught me nothing else but *patience is a virtue*, then it was all worth it. The best things take time. Run the meter. Make the client pay. The longer something takes, the more rewarded you are—in my profession, anyway. Keep 'em on the line; keep 'em dangling. Get all the facts. Plan ahead. Make your case. Details, details, details. People, places, prioritize. Work at it. Long days and even longer nights. Track and taste revenge right on the tip of your tongue. Addresses and credit scores. Salaries and bonuses, employment and eviction notices. I knew every fucking thing about those three bastards. I knew where they shopped and slept and ate. Who and when they fucked. When they would shit and piss. Which bar they frequented. I knew all their past and current employers—low level construction jobs, mostly…those brain-dead fucktards couldn't land a decent paying gig for the life of them. Yard grunts. Construction site nail pickers. Freemont: stucco; Cook: house painter; Underwood: unemployed, currently living on WCB cheques because he fell off a ladder (or some bullshit) while carrying shingles for a roofing company.

And all three right here, right now. Not thirty yards from where I stood.

Blood rushed through my body. Adrenaline blasted through my veins as I anticipated what the next torturous hours would bring. I walked in confidence. In a I-am-the-fucking-boss-right-now-so-you-better-listen stride. Face to face. Three against one…

"Good evening, gentlemen," I said. All three stared in disbelief. Their drinks in hand.

"Well if it isn't our little Blossom…Fuck me." Underwood: the smug, cocky fool looked at each of his mates. They smirked in disbelief.

I pushed my jacket to the side and put my hand in my pocket, exposing not only my holstered 9mm but also Alex's badge that was clipped to my belt. "I need you three to come with me," I said.

A pause—one that determined the rest of their lives. Would they walk away and laugh? Would they sucker punch me? Or would they listen and obey? Do as I say.

"What the hell is this?" Underwood said. "What're you doing?" He had to shout a little now because the music blared and drowned out voices with a wave of bass and treble.

I slid my hand out of my pocket, snapped open the safety clip on the holster, and placed my hand on the gun. "You need to turn around and leave the building"—I said, pointing toward the back exit—"right now." Nobody around us noticed what the hell was going on. They were too busy grinding and jumping and laughing. "Turn Down for What" by Lil Jon thumped through the speakers. The stage lights flickered red, blue, green, yellow—a strobe light pulsated and made everything look like slow motion. I thought Underwood was going to take a swing at me. But amazingly he looked at each of his bros and said, "Let's get this over with."

I couldn't believe it! This might actually work!

Okay…stay calm…stay focused.

I followed them as they shuffled out. None of them were in a hurry to go anywhere. Robert rammed the door handle hard and pushed it open. The cool air hit our faces, a stark contrast from the heat and sweat of the gym.

The door slammed shut behind us. The dark parking lot was empty. A full moon hovered above, illuminating our faces. I pulled out my cell phone and sent a text. Robert, Jeremy, and Michael looked at each other in confusion.

Jeremy, the ever brave one, said, "Listen, Blossom, what's this about? We'd like to move on here…"

"So you're a cop, huh?" Robert said. "Doesn't look right. You're not big enough."

I kept my cool. I texted again.

"Why you keep lookin' at your phone?" Underwood said as he took a big step toward me. His movement subconsciously signaled the other two to follow. "Let me see your badge again—"

A white Ford Econoline van screeched into the parking lot and stopped a few feet away. The bright halogen headlights blinded my three would be assaulters. The driver, passenger, and rear doors opened: four of the biggest, baddest, most brutally insane, leather-clad bikers jumped out. They were all full patch members of The Hosts of Hell Motorcycle Club and were clients of mine. And built like NFL linebackers. Trashcan Stan got his nickname because he eats everything and anything, even a human or two, if required. He was completely bald, no neck, his arms covered in jailhouse tattoos. Loser Lou was a degenerate gambler who owed money to a couple of Russian mob guys a few years back. Instead of paying them he blew up one of their houses and torched a bar they liked to frequent. He stood the tallest, with long black hair that reached down the centre of his back. Frankie The Fuck was a sex addict with an insatiable and voracious appetite for women; he could fuck three, four, five women a night and still get it up. He looked like a male model. He had strong, high cheekbones and gorgeously thick blond hair with the body of a Crossfit champion. All he wore was a leather vest that showed off his chiseled abs. Finally, there was John The Pimp. He was about six foot seven, 265 or 270 pounds, depending on how much jewelry he wore. He usually had a ring on each finger, some of them blood stained.

All faced major jail time but got off scot-free and had their fees waived. "I'll take your muscles in lieu of payment," I said to them. Confused, yet grateful that their money stayed in their pockets, they obliged my request.

"These the guys?" Trashcan asked. He was inches away from Underwood's face. Underwood was shaken and the drink in his hand fell to the ground. The bottle smashed and drops of beer hit on Stan's black leather boots. "Get on your knees and lick that off—right now!"

Underwood wasn't sure what to do—he looked at Jeremy and Robert for help. They were dumbfounded; frozen stiff. Scared—yes, SCARED!

"NOW—MOTHERFUCKER!"

Without further protest, Underwood got down on his hands and knees and licked every last drop of Heineken off Trashcan Stan's boots.

I couldn't believe my eyes. Indeed, revenge, was so very, very sweet…

Oh, but the *real* fun was just about to begin…

"Why are you doing this?" Jeremy said.

John The Pimp slammed his fist into Freemont's chest. He doubled over and collapsed to the floor, wheezing and gagging, unable to breathe properly.

Trashcan Stan kicked Underwood in the face as hard as he could and knocked the poor son of a bitch right out. Robert Cook made a mad dash for the door, but Frankie The Fuck tripped him; he hit the pavement. Frankie kicked Cook in the ribs a few times for good measure. I could hear the courage seep out of him…

My guys picked all three of them up and threw them into the back of the van. I rode shotgun and Trashcan Stan drove. John and Frankie and Lou all rode in the back.

Underwood, Cook, and Freemont were now fish in my barrel. Trashcan backed out of the parking lot, made a couple of turns, and drove away from Burnaby Central Senior Secondary. I could almost hear the accelerated beat of their hearts; their adrenal glands punched the clock and worked overtime.

And then when I picked up my cell phone and dialed Alex's number and asked her if she was "at the warehouse," all the bravado and machismo bullshit left their bodies. They were no longer bullies: they were now *The Bullied*.

CHAPTER 7:

Grade 12 (1996-1997)

By the time Labour Day came around, I was what some might consider a full-blown alcoholic. The vodka and 7-Up concoction Alex introduced me to seemed to be my latest crutch. I realized I could drink pretty much anywhere and Mom never smelled a thing (that may have been because her and Sergiu drank heavily, too, and it masked my own sins). My grandparents—who I barely saw these days—didn't suspect anything either. I usually only saw them when I went to pick up my sister after a Sunday spent with gramps. Sometimes I smoked a little weed, but it made me paranoid. I spent a couple of afternoons on the couch, shaking and shivering, my blood sugar level all fucked up. I preferred the drink. It was easier to "control."

My marks were almost perfect the previous year. I had 96–98% in most courses and I could probably achieve higher if I just gave it a little extra push. I knew if I maintained anything above 95% almost any university in Canada (and most in the USA) would welcome me with open arms, especially with my soccer achievements.

It was the Friday before the start of school and I was on the field with the rest of my team, buzzed and happy. Coach Rocca discussed potential scholarships, scouts attending our games, and the importance of giving it our all this year and making it the "best year yet."

The grass was still wet with morning dew and it started to soak my shorts. Most of the team stood, but I had a half and half mixture of vodka and seven in a 500 ml plastic bottle I sipped from and I didn't feel like standing.

Coach Rocca wanted us to run a few drills and play a mini-game (there was sixteen of us present, so eight per side). We did not have to "try out," as it were, because in Grade 12, it was all about the invite.

I noticed a tall, fit kid with dark black curly hair and a Spanish accent, like Antonio Banderas, who was also among us. I had never seen him before.

"Okay, boys," Coach Rocca said, "before we begin, I'd like to introduce Carlos Cardoza. He just moved here from sunny Guatemala, and I'd like you all to welcome him aboard." We clapped half-heartedly. Nobody liked a new guy. A threat. "He played for his high school team and for one of the colleges last year. So, I know he'll be a great addition to our team and our program here at Central."

Carlos smiled and gave a little wave. He wore a pair of white Umbro shorts—a big no-no, only the girls wore those—and a T-shirt with a big blue Nike swoosh on the front. It had a hole in it and looked second-hand.

Coach Rocca split up the teams and we kicked off. Carlos played right mid-field and within the first twenty minutes he ran circles around me. I couldn't keep up. I was out of breath and dizzy. The alcohol seemed to hit me even harder the more I ran.

And then I puked. Right after I took a big shot from just outside the penalty box (it went wide) I bent over and hurled. Big splashes of partially digested eggs and bacon and bread and booze came tumbling out. What a fucking nightmare.

"You all right?" Rocca asked.

"I'll be okay," I said.

"Take a knee," he told me after he blew his whistle.

I bent down and put my hand on my forehead. I really didn't feel well.

I coughed and hacked, but no vomit. Coach Rocca was up close to me know. "Stand up," he said. "Come with me." We walked across the field toward the school and the cement bleachers. He yelled, "Everybody keep playing," and held my arm tight around my right bicep. We were now off

A BULLIED REUNION

the field. "You smell like my grandfather's liquor cabinet. What the fuck's the matter with you?"

My whole world went silent. I could hear my heart in my head. And then the voices and questions and demons stormed through—

I thought you couldn't smell vodka. I thought—I mean—I—why did he ask me?

"It's ten-thirty and you smell like the bar," he said.

"I went to a party last night," I said.

I hoped that covered it but he was too smart for his or my own good. He walked over to —oh fuck oh fuck oh shit oh fuck—and unscrewed the cap. I was done. I was fucked. He smelled it, unsure, and then took a sip. His eyes pronounced my doom. He pounded toward me, carrying the bottle in front of him like a nest of bees.

"What is this?" he asked. "You been drinkin' this all morning?"

I could not face him. I stared down at the ground, ashamed.

"Sorry," was all I could manage. The sun was hot on the back of my neck. I was sweaty and sick.

"Sorry isn't gonna cut it," he said. "This is serious. What the hell were you thinking, huh?" He blew his whistle again and called everybody in. He screwed the cap back on and held the bottle in his right hand.

"All right," he said to the team, "that's enough for today. School starts next week and so does practice. Tuesdays and Wednesdays. Right here. That last bell rings, you live on this field for the next eight months, got it?"

"Yes, sir!" the team shouted in unison.

"Off you go," he said.

A couple of players stayed back to speak with him, but he shooed them away and said, "Some other time, guys. I need a moment with Cris right now." They may have thought he was favouring his star player…if they only knew…

Rocca's voice sounded like the teacher on *Charlie Brown* to me: just a bunch of honks and horns and useless vowels, syllables and sentences that were jumbled together. He just kept on and on and on while I looked him in the face. All I could think was *is he going to give me my bottle back?* I wanted another drink, badly. Miss Diamond's face popped up in my head every time

I looked over at the school. What did she look like with a pregnant belly? Did she cut her hair? Did she like her new school? Was there someone else?

"So, if this happens again, you're done, okay?" Coach Rocca said, and this time I heard him. I guess my brain listened subconsciously and knew when the end was coming.

"It won't happen again," I said. It wasn't very convincing, mind you.

"You never know which game a scout will show up to. And it could mean everything. Your whole future is decided in this last year of school." He clasped his hands behind his back. "Look, I know your father passed away and things aren't perfect at home, but this is not the way to cope."

Coach Rocca and I had been through a lot. We'd won and lost, laughed and cried, both in victory and defeat, and I know he expected more of me; I did not want to let him down. If there was any man left alive I truly wanted to make proud, it was him.

"I've been drinking a lot this summer," I said, "but I'm done. I promise."

With that, he grabbed me under my armpits and stood me up. "I know you are." He patted me on the back and we walked side-by-side to the main entrance. "You okay to get home?" he asked, the bottle still firmly gripped in his hand.

"Yeah, I'm good," I said.

"I'll see you Tuesday," he said with a nod and a wink. Then he threw the bottle in the garbage without dumping the contents. I waved and walked away. But once I heard the front doors close, I turned around, grabbed the bottle out of the trash can, and quickly ran to the bus stop. I gulped down the other half within about a minute, let out a big burp, and felt normal again.

Sorry, Coach.

* * *

Alex—in her own mysteriously connected way—arranged for us to be locker partners for the fifth straight year. Now that we were in our last year, most of our classes were on the first floor along with our lockers. It was a privilege given to senior students: after climbing those dreaded stairs for four years, we could now take comfort in the fact that everything we needed was on the main level.

I hung my backpack on the hook and said, "You taking Drama again this year?"

She hung up her own pack and replied, "It's an easy A. Why not?"

I placed my bottle of vodka and seven on the upper shelf.

"Are you serious with that?" Alex said. "Like, come on."

Since she attended that Junior Police Academy thing over the summer she had become somewhat of a Miss Goody Two-Shoes. She had told me how stringent the selection process was: they not only do a background check but also a psychological examination, an interview, and the dreaded lie detector test. So, she had to "keep her nose clean" for the rest of the year and seriously consider her life.

In a nutshell, Alex was now a bore…but she was still my Alex. Forever best buds.

"I'm weaning off," I said.

"Wean a little faster. And not during school. You get caught with that and we're both in deep shit."

"It's mine. You have nothing to worry about."

She cared for me. Deeply.

"All right," she said. "I'll see you in a few—"

The first period bell rang. I grabbed my binder and headed for Block A. Math or Chemistry or something or other…fuck if I knew…

Lunch could not come fast enough. It was the longest half-day in the history of academia. I shivered and shook and sweated through all the classes. When that final bell rang I ran to my locker, gulped down the last quarter of my drink, and felt the warmth and calm overtake me.

Coach Rocca saw me take the big, long gulp and was suspicious, I was sure. My heart was easily at two hundred and my head spun with fear, but he just walked on by, gave me a thumbs up. I shoved the bottle into my bag and slammed the locker shut. I'd talk to Alex later. I had to get out of here, fast.

"Hey, there, buddy boy," Michael Underwood, now easily the tallest twelfth grader in the entire school—maybe the entire district—was right up in my face, with Jeremy Freemont and his fucking partner, Robert Cook. "Where're you rushing off to?"

"Look, I don't have time for your shit right now, okay?" I said.

"*My* shit?" he said. "You'll eat *my* shit if I tell you to." He slammed my shoulders into the locker.

I didn't get where this was coming from. Wasn't he worried I'd report him?

"What's this about?" I asked. They circled me and I couldn't see beyond them. They towered over me like a pack of bridge trolls. There were a bunch of students around, all noisy and distracted with their own lives, not interested in mine whatsoever.

"This is about you knowing who's who and what's what," Underwood said. "Mr. Price is no longer around. He's gone. There's nobody here to protect you."

They took a step closer. I saw Alex out of the corner of my eye, walking fast and hard. She had some sort of wooden candy cane shaped stick.

"And I think for the rest of the year," Underwood began, "you need to pay us a school tax." He looked to the others and they smiled. I had heard through the grapevine they had been doing this to a few of the other (weaker) students over the past year. "Every Friday you better have two crisp twenty-dollar bills ready for me, or else everything's gonna hurt."

"What? You think you're the mafia?"—I giggled a little here—"You're an idiot, that's what you are," I slurred.

Alex was only a few feet away now; I could see her over Freemont's left shoulder. She was holding her stick in a baseball swing position. She let it rip, connecting with the back of Jeremy Freemont's knees. He collapsed in pain and screamed. She then swung and hit Underwood squarely in the jaw, knocking him out cold. Robert Cook was smart (and fast) enough to run the other way the moment the whole ordeal went down.

Coach Rocca stepped out of the classroom just as Alex stood over both Underwood and Freemont. She said, "Don't you ever talk to my fucking friend again!"

"Hey! Hey! Whoa!" Rocca said as he grabbed Alex's grass hockey stick. "What the hell is going on?!" He panicked when he saw Underwood on the ground, completely out. His legs shook, and he looked as if he was having a seizure. "Call the nurse!" Rocca yelled. "Hurry!"

Freemont slid back against one of the lockers and held his knee. "What the fuck is the matter with you?" he said to Alex.

"Shut your mouth," Alex replied.

A BULLIED REUNION

"Both of you—enough," Rocca said. He was over Underwood now; he gently slapped his face to wake him up…nothing. His jaw looked funny. It was angled differently; off-centre. It looked broken.

Shit.

The nurse finally showed up. She was a short Asian lady who wore a black Puma track suit. She put on a pair of latex gloves. She cracked smelling salts under Underwood's nose and waved it around. He came to, but he could not speak. He just mumbled and drooled.

"We need to call an ambulance," the nurse said.

Coach Rocca nodded and ran to the main offices like the athlete he was. "Stay down," the nurse said to Underwood, "don't get up."

Alex and I looked at each other and shrugged, but I knew she was in deep shit. This was assault, not self-defense. They hadn't done anything to me, except verbally threaten.

Fuck.

"Head home," said the nurse, shooing everyone away.

Moments later, Coach Rocca was back. He said, "They're on their way. You, go to the office, right now," he said to Alex.

"They were gonna hurt my friend," she said. "I was just protecting him." She stood where she was and protested Rocca's command to go to the office.

"I don't have time for this right now—just go. Leave."

Underwood mumbled something—but it was unclear, muffled. He was on his back. Tears streamed from his eyes. He was clearly in pain.

Good.

Alex grabbed her backpack and took off.

"She's had enough," I said to Coach Rocca. "And so have I."

"This is not the answer," Rocca said. He pulled me aside and my back was up against the locker. "That kid's jaw is probably broken—"

"He threatened me," I said. "He said if I don't give him forty bucks every Friday he'd hurt me."

Coach Rocca let out a big breath, turned around, and rubbed his head. He ruffled his hair and paced. The paramedics showed up, stabilized Underwood's neck, moved him onto a gurney, and wheeled him out of the school. He gave me the finger as he rolled away.

"You see that?" I said to Coach Rocca. "That guy's pure fucking evil."

It was just him and I now. Freemont had left before the paramedics showed up.

"My brother's a prison guard and I'm a teacher," Rocca said to me. "But some days I don't know the difference…"

* * *

Alex was suspended for two weeks. If it wasn't for her father threatening to sue, and a couple of students who had seen all three boys intimidate me, she would have been expelled. The next two weeks went by in a flash. Underwood, his jaw broken and wired shut, was gone for a week. Tupac Shakur—whose music Alex had introduced me to over the summer—had been shot in Las Vegas right after the Mike Tyson vs. Bruce Seldon fight. He died six days later and seven months to the day of the release of "All Eyez On Me"—an album I had on repeat in my Sony Discman. Indeed, Mr. Price was no longer the principal, as I would find out at our yearly assembly. (I once again received an award for my soccer and scholastic endevours.) Our new fearless leader was Mr. McNally, a red-haired ex-cop who was around sixty but looked like he just turned forty. He was in exceptional shape, with arms the size of tree trunks and shoulders that struggled to fit through doors. He was a teacher until he joined the Vancouver Police Department at thirty-five. He retired after twenty years and went back to teaching, where he was promoted to principal within five years. I knew Alex would be excited to pick his brain once she returned from her suspension—which, I thought, may now affect her chances of being accepted into the force.

On the morning that Alex returned, Mr. McNally summoned both of us to his office.

"Have a seat," he said. Alex sat to my right. The office was as if Mr. Price had never left. Except for the pictures on the wall and a new set of books on the shelf behind him, everything looked the same: static and monotonous. The coolest thing, though, was a big picture on the wall to the left of Mr. McNally. It showed six Emergency Response Team (like SWAT) officers lined up against a brick wall, ready to penetrate a building, weapons—Heckler & Koch MP5 sub-machine guns, Glocks, and a shotgun—at the ready.

Helmets, balaclavas, boots, and leather gloves, vests with extra ammo, and specialized radios covered their massive bodies. The bottom of the picture was signed by each member of the team—including Mr. McNally, who spent five years as an ERT officer.

"That's a cool picture," I said. "Which one are you?"

"Second guy, behind the shield," Mr. McNally replied.

Alex couldn't look away.

"You like that?" he asked her.

"Yeah," she said, "it's actually my dream."

"To join the ERT?"

"To be a cop."

"Well, young lady, what transpired a couple of weeks ago is *not* going to help the cause, I can tell you that much. The VPD is not looking for violent offenders. And what you did was unacceptable. Personally, I thought you would have been expelled, but the school board thought otherwise. I'm not saying you blew your chance, but what you do from now on will go a long way. Because when you apply, they'll not only talk to me, but also to each one of your teachers, your parents, some of your friends—and even your enemies. They'll dig so deep they'll find people in your life *you* didn't even know existed."

Alex swallowed hard, but she never took her eyes off Mr. McNally.

"And that's why I've called you both in today," he said. "I want us to have a great year. The best one you've ever had. And I want to put this fiasco behind us. I know why you did what you did, Alex. And a part of me—off the record—admires your loyalty and the way you stood up for your friend. That goes a long way in life. But—and there is always a BUT—I don't ever want to hear your name again unless it's on an award or follows an academic accolade."

Alex nodded.

"And now you, sir," he said to me, "are another story all together…"

I looked up at the clock: recess would be over in seven minutes.

"Look at me when I'm talking to you," Mr. McNally said.

I'd only had a few sips this morning…well, maybe a bit more…and I desperately wanted a big gulp right now. My body shook a little. I was nervous.

"We need to change a few things," he said; "because I know *everything*…"

He leaned forward on his desk, hands clasped together. "I know what happened in the past—I spoke to all of your teachers. I've looked at your school file and I think I understand you pretty well." Alex stared at me. "I know the issues you've had with Underwood, Freemont and"—he looked into the manila folder on his desk—"Mr. Cook. I need you to tell me each time a problem arises. I don't want either of you dealing with this on your own. Got it? You need to come to me. As does every other student that may have a problem, whether it's with bullying or whatever the case. I am here for you. Okay?"

I looked at Alex. Her face said she had nothing to say or add. I could tell she felt as though the less she said, the better she would fare. So, I piped up.

"I appreciate this, Mr. McNally. I really do. I don't know what I've done to make them hate me so much."

"You did nothing. Absolutely nothing," he said. "Maybe something's happening at home; maybe there's abuse, who knows? It's in their nature to bully. And it's in mine to break them if they do. I've got my eye on those three, don't you worry. All you need to do is keep your head down, study hard, and bring in the grades. You both have a bright future. Don't do anything stupid to mess it up."

I went straight to my locker and chucked my bottle of vodka and seven. I told myself I would never touch alcohol again. I even spoke to Coach Rocca at the end of the day, right before soccer practice, and told him some of my struggles. He understood, and knew something was amiss, but was ill-equipped to deal with everyone's issues and inner battles. It was good. I felt as though something fresh was beginning.

As Halloween rolled around, my grades and projects were exceptional, my brain felt lighter, and my step was quicker since I dropped the drink. But best of all: neither one of the Stooges bothered Alex or me! It was like they completely disappeared. We saw them from time to time in the hallway, but they would literally walk the other way when either of us approached. I think it was because Mr. McNally policed the hallways like the officer he used to be. He paced up and down, peeked into classrooms every so often, and made his presence known to all. During recess and lunch, he was always up and about, conversing with students, shooting hoops, and high-fiving the grade eights in the cafeteria, making them feel welcome. He was just an all-around nice guy, who cared for our welfare. We all felt safe. Secure. Free to be ourselves.

But in my world, when one thing was up, another was down. When part of my life was going right, the other part would swerve left.

"Hey, I need to talk to you," Alex said. We were at our locker, about to head to the cafeteria.

"What's up?" I asked, curious.

Alex looked at the ground, her hands empty and folded across her stomach. "Well…you know how Mrs. Barnes and I are good friends, right?"

"Yeah," I replied. *Where was this going?*

"I just spoke to her a few minutes ago. She's helping me fill out my college application. And we got to talking…. I'm not sure how her name came up, but one thing led to another and she gave me some bad news."

Before she said it, I knew.

"I hate to be the one to tell you this, but I don't think anybody else will," Alex said.

"Just tell me," I said impatiently.

Alex swallowed hard. "She killed herself."

My ears rang loudly, and my head felt warm and fuzzy. My stomach went hollow and it was as if someone had sucked the air out of my lungs.

I didn't have to ask "Who?" or "What?" or "When?" I knew. So, all I asked was "How?"

"I don't really know the details, but, apparently, she took a buncha pills and drank a bottle of whiskey."

I thought I might throw up. I gagged and turned around, facing the inside of my locker. I felt Alex's hand on my back. She said, "She lost the baby and I guess it all went downhill from there…I dunno…"

I had zero contact with Miss Diamond. I only knew that she was somewhere in Abbotsford which, to me, might as well have been fucking Nova Scotia. I tried to forget everything about her. I buried our time together deep. It was the only way to move on and cope. Otherwise I'd still be a fucking mess. Which I was now…

I went from hot to cold and I shivered. I shook with my head inside the locker. And then I threw up in the garbage can a few feet away. Principal McNally happened to walk by and asked, "Are you okay?"

"He just heard some bad news…" Alex said.

"Come see me if you need to," he said. I was still bent over the can. I nodded. He patted my back and kept on. Most adults would stay and talk, but McNally wasn't like that. He knew how to give space.

I wiped my mouth with my sleeve and said, "I think I'm gonna go home."

"I think you should…and I'm sorry. Maybe I shouldn't've told you yet, but I just couldn't—"

"You did the right thing… I needed to know."

Alex looked me in the eye. "I don't need you getting all fucked up over this, okay? You're NOT drinking."

I nodded.

"Promise me," she said.

"I promise," I said.

She gave me a big hug and I cried a little. I grabbed my backpack and headed to the office. I told the secretary I wasn't feeling well, and I needed to go home. Mr. McNally was there photocopying something and nodded his head in agreement. I pushed through the front doors and burst into tears.

I walked to the exact same bench in Deer Lake Park where I first kissed Miss Diamond. It was the spot where we gave birth to our love. Just as I sat down on the cold, hard, wooden seat and said the word "birth" in my mind, the tears flowed again. My mouth contorted, and my face was a wretched mess of pain and distress. I wanted to see her face again; I wanted to touch her skin ever so badly. I wanted to… I just wanted—Her. But she was gone now. Like the cliché, she took a piece of my heart. I just sat and wallowed in the mire of my own pain. Subconsciously, I reached into my backpack and tried to grab my vodka and seven, but it was not there, which was probably a good thing.

I walked around the lake aimlessly for the next hour or so. I veered off the path every so often and kicked trees and threw rocks. My sorrow turned into anger, rage, fury. I hated my heart for betraying me. I hated myself for falling, for loving, and for living—

I cried myself dry that night. My lungs and abdominals were sore and spent from continually contracting. I slept in and missed first period. I showed up to school just before recess and nobody cared. The world kept going on at its pace without Miss Diamond, like it didn't even matter. Like her existence was insignificant. I just wanted to press PAUSE on the world for a moment and let everyone know how special and important she was to me. I decided to speak with Mrs. Barnes. I wanted to ask her if she knew when or where the funeral or memorial service was being held.

"I'll take you if you like," she said when I caught her in the hallway and asked. "Maybe Alex would like to come, too?"

"Yeah, I think she would," I said. "And thank you. I appreciate it."

The service was at *Living Word Pentecostal Assembly* in Abbotsford. From what I heard, her parents were big time holy rollers who attended this bible-thumping, hell-fire, speaking in tongues church. It would be the opposite of what Miss Diamond would want as a final funeral service but also somewhat fitting because she was crazy in her own beautiful way. I could see how growing up with the nuttiness of a charismatic church could make someone not only run the other way but embrace everything about life that was NOT of that world. She clearly lived her life by her own rules—and at times I think she made them up as she went along.

"Could you meet me in front of the school around noon?" Mrs. Barnes asked. She was short and skinny and had long, black, hippy-type hair, with the part directly in the middle. Her clothes were bought second-hand at Value Village so she could put her money aside for trips to Costa Rica, Mexico, Brazil, and other exotic locations. She loved backpacking, hiking, drinking hallucinogenic teas and herbal concoctions, while smoking grass and taking pictures of places where running water was a complete luxury.

"Yeah, that's fine," I said. "Alex and I'll jump on the bus and meet you here."

She gave me a big hug. She smelled like mold but she was nice and gentle and stroked my face. "I know you were very close to her," she said. "I know all about you two…she spoke often of your love…and I think it was beautiful and healthy." Then she came in really close, put her hand on my shoulder, and looked up at me. "Love makes us come alive. But it can also be cruel and difficult and unfair. Love is both our friend *and* our enemy."

I think I knew what she meant by love being our enemy. I was glad when she left but angry that she was privy to our secret. I thought Miss Diamond, Alex and I were the only ones who knew. *Who else did she tell?*

*   *   *

Other than my father's, I had only been to one other memorial service in my life. It was for a friend of my mom's a few years back. I didn't know the person, so I was basically emotionally unattached. But Miss Diamond's memorial was something I would remember for the rest of my life...

The massive white building had this wooden cross on the peak. People dressed in expensive suits and yellow and orange reflector vests guided cars into their parking stalls. Everyone smiled and shook hands with us when we entered the main sanctuary. *Aren't you supposed to be sad and sombre? Why the fuck are you smiling? A woman killed herself!*

They played what was called "worship music" in the background while people found their seats. To pay their respects to Miss Diamond, they took a quick moment of silence as they stood next to a picture of her that sat on a table. There was also a bouquet of flowers and a Bible open to (apparently) her favourite scripture verse, which was highlighted in yellow. The print was bright red and it sounded as though someone was speaking: "*I am the resurrection, and the life: he that believeth in me, though he were dead, yet shall he live.*"

The pews were padded and long. They were completely different from the Romanian Orthodox churches I'd attended in the past. There were no religious icons, stained glass windows, or incense burning; just a mess of musical instruments—drums, guitars on stands, a baby grand piano, an electric keyboard, and three elevated rows for the choir—and a large wooden pulpit (the same colour as the cross on the roof) that had a lion's head carved into it.

We sat in the fifth row. I couldn't bring myself to go to the front and look at her picture. I wondered where the body was. In most Orthodox services the casket was open for viewing but these people seemed to have their own way of doing things—

"Everyone, please take your seats," a sturdy man said from the front. His voice was amplified by a microphone on his lapel. "I'd like to thank you all for coming here today. I know the family appreciates your support during this difficult time."

The man read a bunch of verses and a few people in the crowd responded with "Amen" and "Glory." It was odd to hear this interaction between preacher and parishioner because I was taught to keep quiet and still. Then Miss Diamond's father stood up and talked about how Miss Diamond used to swim for hours and hours as a child, how she loved to teach Sunday school when she was a teenager, how she dedicated her life to God and his work, and how she never took on a husband or boyfriend. *So how do you explain the pregnancy, pal?* He talked about how everyone in life will make mistakes, but "God sees the heart. He knows our motives and is all loving and all powerful. His forgiveness is eternal. There is nothing we can do that can separate us from his grace. Amen."

Mr. Diamond sat down. Then Miss Diamond's niece approached the stage, grabbed a microphone, and sang "It Is Well My Soul." I don't know if it was the music, the pain, the sorrow, or the plain stupidity that encompassed my life from time to time, but when the pastor asked if there was anybody else that wanted to say a few words, I was the first one to get up and speak.

I walked up the carpeted steps and stood behind the pulpit but that didn't feel right. So, I grabbed a microphone from the stand the previous singer used. Alex looked at me as though I had completely lost my fucking mind.

"Lena and I loved each other. It was my baby she carried." It was like I was in some sort of protective bubble. Like nobody could touch or hurt me. The big, bright stage lights made me feel as though I was in total control of the room. The faces of those in the crowd—that numbered around two hundred—were in shock. Lena's parents looked as though someone told them that Jesus was sitting at their dining table waiting for them to return home: absolute shock and disbelief. I looked directly at the crowd and continued, "Her heart was truly made of gold. And her soul, like her last name, was a priceless diamond: perfect in every way and rare and flawless and bright and shiny and—" I choked up. "—and I miss her terribly."

I placed the microphone back into the stand. My hand shook, and I felt an enormous adrenaline dump. I walked down the steps and faced her picture. The crowd behind me was still in silent shock. I reached deep into my pocket and removed the monthly pass to the aquatic centre that Lena had given me all those years ago and placed it in front of her photo. I kissed two fingers and touched them to her smiling lips. I walked up the aisle and out of the building. Alex and Mrs. Barnes quickly followed.

* * *

Numb.

It was like anesthesia was running through my veins ever since the memorial. It was not from any drink or drug, pill or potion. It was as if an elixir entered my body and created this divide between myself and the rest of society. I spoke only when spoken to, answered only when asked, and moved only when necessary.

Minutes and hours and days and classes and soccer games and homework and university applications and acceptances all came and went in a snap. Life presented itself on a conveyor belt and I took what I needed and left the rest.

Alex knew well enough to leave me be. She was soaked in the volunteer work and extra-curricular activities needed in order to beef-up her submission to the Justice Institute of BC.

I, on the other hand, was accepted to the University of British Columbia, where I would complete my bachelor's in criminology before entering the UBC Allard School of Law. I wasn't sure why law was my thing. I thought about the Creative Writing program—all my English teachers said that was a much better path and more well suited for a "brooding writer" such as myself; but I when I took *Introduction to Law* as my Grade 12 elective, I immediately fell in love with verbal combat. It was truly the only time I came out of my protective, anesthetized shell. I felt sedated and slow in the rest of my waking life, but when third period/Block **C** came around, I lit up like a Christmas tree.

As I sat in that very classroom and packed up my books to head out to my Block D (Math 12) class, life once again would go *left* when I tried to steer everything *right*.

It was Monday, February 17 at 1:55 p.m., and I had been summoned to the office…

Mr. McNally sat at his desk and motioned for me to sit down.

"I sent a message to Miss Deliano that you might not be in her class this afternoon," he said. He was sombre, sad.

I immediately knew that Alex was in trouble. She had not shown up for school, and when I tried to call her house at lunch, there was no answer.

"Alex will need you as a friend more than ever right now," he said.

A BULLIED REUNION

A lump in my throat instantly materialized. Mr. McNally could not even face me. He just stared at his ERT picture on the wall.

"She's going to be fine," he said, "but she'll need our help."

I swallowed. "What happened?"

"She went to a Valentine's Day party on Friday night"—his lips trembled as he spoke—"and sometime after midnight, she was raped by a group of boys."

"What…?" was all my mind could manage.

"She was hurt pretty bad. We don't know who they were and nobody at the party seems to remember or wants to come forward."

As an ex-cop, I was sure he had dealt with much worse than this, but he was visibly upset. I knew he had developed a close mentorship with Alex, helping with her applications to the Justice Institute and even writing her a reference.

"Where is she now?" I asked.

"She's still in the hospital. They knocked her unconscious and beat her up pretty bad." He paused. "I'm going to visit her tonight…I thought you might want to come."

Of course I did! But more than that, I wanted to know who the fuck did this to her. And why? Everyone loved Alex—

And then a wave of knowing, of pure assurance, hit me square in the face. Those fuckers. Those fucking motherfuckers!

"I know who it was," I said.

"Who?" Mr. McNally replied, confused.

"I think it's pretty obvious…" I was bent over now, elbows on knees, eyes to the ground.

"If you know anything—we need to go to the police right now."

"I know…" I said. "They wore condoms, right?"

Mr. McNally was taken back. "How do you know that?" he asked me.

"Because this was *planned*. It wasn't a spur of the moment thing. If it was, they wouldn't *all* have rubbers."

He leaned back in his chair and saw what I saw. Thought what I thought.

"There's no blood, no sperm. No proof that they even did it, right?" I said knowingly.

He nodded his head.

CHRIS PONICI

"Michael Underwood, Robert Cook, and Jeremy Freemont raped and assaulted Alex," I said.

*   *   *

My mind was made up. At 2:30 that afternoon, while classes were still in session, I was going to avenge Alex. I would kill. Murder. And like the Metallica song that played through my Sony Walkman I would—

"Seek and Destroy."

*   *   *

She was pale. Sickly. Jaundiced and just barely awake. Her right eye was swollen shut and her lips were inflated and pillowy. Blood crusted on her forehead and scabs circled her cheeks. There were teeth marks on her neck where one of the assailants had taken a bite out of her! The room was dark and there were three other patients across from her with their drapes drawn. Mr. McNally and I hovered over the bed. I touched her arm. She was cold. Unresponsive.

"Alex," I whispered.

Nothing.

The nurse said we could visit, but that Alex might be asleep. She gave her a sedative an hour ago. From his former cop years, he knew all the staff at the hospital. He had interviewed many a victim in their beds, so the nurse said it would be okay for us to "hang out a bit."

It was almost eight o'clock and dark outside. Her window had a view of a brick wall.

"I'm gonna hurt them…and they're gonna feel pain like never before," I said. But it wasn't to Alex nor to Mr. McNally, and not even to myself. I wasn't sure who I said it to, I just did. Words kept coming out of my mouth. "I'm gonna pull their fingernails out one by one. I'm gonna break their arms, toes, ankles, knees. Each and every fucking rib. Then I'll gut them like pigs…"

"Cris—" McNally said. But I kept on.

"I'll burn their bodies and send the ashes to their mothers."

Alex opened her good eye. "Would you shut up?" she mumbled through her blood-stained lips. "You're not doing anything."

My pulse quickened. "Alex," I said.

"Yeah?"

"Are you okay?"

"Never better…can't you tell?" She smiled, more with her eyes than lips; her nose crinkled.

She then looked over to Mr. McNally and a tear immediately slid down her cheek. "I'm sorry," she said. It was just like Alex to apologize for getting hurt. "Is this gonna affect—"

"Alex," Mr. McNally said, "this is NOT your fault. Okay?" He sat down next to her on the bed and moved in close. "We need you to tell us who did this…"

Alex looked up at me. Her lips were closed tight. Defiant.

"No," she said. "It's my problem. I'll deal with it."

"Alex—you need to—" McNally tried.

"I said NO," she winced in pain.

Mr. McNally looked at me. I shrugged my shoulders a bit. Just enough to say, *that's Alex. She doesn't need anyone…*

"Okay…you get some rest. When you're feeling better, you can talk to the police."

Alex was stone still.

Mr. McNally got up, patted her covered leg, looked at me, and said, "I'll be in the lounge. Take your time."

I nodded as he walked way.

"I'm not telling them anything," Alex said.

"I know."

"We're gonna do this thing. For both of us. For all the shit that's gone down." She took a deep breath in through her nose. "Maybe not today. Maybe not tomorrow. But one day…"

I held her hand gently. "One day."

CHAPTER 8:

Twenty Year High School Reunion (2017)

Alex chose the place.

She worked a three month case that led to a major bust at a cocaine distribution warehouse at the end of Alexander Street in the downtown Eastside. It fronted as a wholesale furniture business that exported goods throughout Canada and the USA after receiving product from abroad.

The building was white with Chinese lettering on the front and the word IMPORTS written on the main door. We entered through the rear, off the alley. There were three padded folding chairs in the middle of the empty warehouse, which only had a few blue metallic shelves—completely empty—lined against the two far, opposite walls. The chairs were home to Michael, Jeremy, and Robert. They were tied back to back so they could not see each other.

A door slammed.

"Well, looky—look," Alex said as she approached. "Aren't you all snuggly..."

"What the fuck is this?!" Underwood yelled. The other two were scared silent. They had not said a word since the school parking lot. "This isn't funny."

(Trashcan) Stan, (Loser) Lou, Frankie (The Fuck), and John (The Pimp) stood in a line, side by side. Alex dropped a huge hockey duffle bag at their feet and unzipped it.

I stepped back and let the boys go to work...

It is quite the sight to see three grown men scream and holler and beg for the pain to stop. You can almost taste their souls leaving their bodies.

The way Stan smashed a crowbar over and over into Robert's stomach and chest, the crack and pop and snap of ribs as they broke and shattered was something to behold. Lou hit a home run every time he swung and connected with Jeremy's kneecaps and shins and ankles—until the bones turned to powder. But—the absofuckinglutely—winner of the night—was when John, after he was done punching Michael in the face with his ringed fists, unzipped Underwood's pants and exposed his thick, black penis.

And then Alex approached.

She had a small butane torch that emitted a flame just big enough to cause painful havoc. Michael squirmed in his seat, his hands tied behind his back, his pants down around his ankles, his right eye swollen shut, his mouth and teeth shattered and broken, his black forehead ripped open, skull exposed. He could lick death. He could taste the end.

"You were a naughty little motherfucker, weren't you?" Alex said, getting right up in his face. "When you fucked me in the ass...when you slapped my mouth and came in my face..." She lowered the blue flame to the tip of his flaccid member and he screamed. His foreskin looked like dark and slimy burned plastic. She kept it there until he cried out and then fainted.

"We're just getting started," Alex said. "Come on, wake up." She used some smelling salts to revive him.

"Pllllllllllleeeeeeeeeeeeeeeeaaaaaaaaaaaaaassssssssseeeeeeeeeeeeeeeeeeee—"

I *almost* felt sorry for the poor bastard...but not really.

"Hey!" Jeremy Freemont was slumped in his seat, his lifeless legs useless and dead. "Just go...just let us go...please...we're sorry..."

Was he for real? Did he actually think this had a happy ending?

John walked over and crushed his fist against the side of Jeremy's skull, right on the ear. It bled like he'd struck oil.

Alex kept on doing her *thing*. She was now on her knees, holding Underwood's testicles in her left hand and the torch in her right. She worked the flame around and around until the skin shriveled to nothing and a small little white sack that looked like an egg fell to the floor. Underwood shook so violently that I thought he would break the chair. His one good eye was rolled back into his head and his toothless mouth gnarled in agony.

Then Alex worked the other one until it, too, fell out. She burned his shaft and kept going over and over and over it until his penis looked like a burnt hot dog.

Underwood passed out again. This time the salts did not bring him back. Alex pulled a Beretta out of her waistband and handed it to me.

"Wanna do the honours?" she said.

I grabbed the gun and pointed it straight at Underwood's destroyed body.

There is no greater high than the moment just before you kill another human being.

Your heart rate increases exponentially. Your eyes become focused and clear; the target the only object of your perfect vision. Your hands tighten around your weapon, ready. Everything moves in slow motion so you can aim and squeeze. Sounds are silenced; deafened ears hear only the breath in your chest, the pressure in your throat as you swallow. Your victim looks you in the eye—and in that final moment, you become GOD.

You are the master of their existence. You decide whether they live or die, whether they leave the earth in suffering or silence. And then the monster wakes after a few minutes and screams one last time and begs for his life. But your mercy has ended. It does not endure.

The smell of shit on your face, the emotional turmoil when your clothes went missing after soccer practice and you were naked and alone in the locker room, the taunting and teasing, the ever-present pressure of pushing and shoving and spitting, the hallway times of terror and classroom crucifixions, the death of a child, the rise of a man...

"Kill that fucker," Alex said.

Underwood gurgled and choked and coughed. I placed the barrel of the gun against his right temple and asked, "How does it feel?"

And then I
sent
him
to
HELL.

The gunshot echoed across the empty warehouse like a hockey puck hitting the boards. I stepped over to Jeremy and looked him in the eyes. He whimpered and shook. His body was a mess of broken bones and bloodied organs. I shot him between the eyes and twice in the stomach.

Stan, Lou, Frankie, and John were already gone. I heard the van start. I put another bullet into the back of Robert's skull. I held the gun at my side and looked at Alex. It all felt sort of anti-climactic. Like there should be more. Like this was too quick. Too easy. Too efficient.

After what felt like a lifetime of torture, it all ended in less than one night. One exhaustively-planned moment. It was done just as quickly as it started and I think we both wanted to feel something. To somehow have a sensation as though a great accomplishment stood before us.

But I felt empty.

Alone.

"Leave 'em here?" Alex said.

I nodded. Nobody would trace this back to us. Alex had taken the gun from the VPD evidence locker. When reported missing, it would be chalked-up to being misfiled or misplaced. No harm, no foul.

I took one last look at Underwood's slumped head. I moved his forehead up with the tip of the barrel and examined his dead face. He would never hurt anybody again. He would never say anything to anyone or touch or breathe or laugh or cry.

I pushed his head all the way so it hung over the back of the chair. I spat on his mouth and cursed. I placed the tip of the weapon against his Adam's apple and pulled the trigger. Meat and blood and spine splattered on my forearm.

With the gun at my side I took Alex by the hand.

She had a look on her weathered face that said:

It. Is. Finished.

CPSIA information can be obtained
at www.ICGtesting.com
Printed in the USA
LVHW03s0044080918
589422LV00001B/3/P